Wally The Worm
And The Great Divide

DJ Michaud

Inimint Press

Cover Art by Tracee Badway
www.traceebadway.com

Cover Design by Steven Novak
www.novakillustration.com

Interior Illustrations by Octavio Jimenez
www.behance.net/moztadio

Author's Note

As a child I was amazed that worms magically appeared when it rained. They covered the sidewalks and streets, placing themselves in harm's way – and there were always the unlucky few who still would be there the next day, shriveled or flattened. Why did they risk their lives to come out in the rain? Exploring this question led to the idea for this book.

I believe that a story should challenge its reader, so purposefully have used words that are a stretch for younger folks. Consider this an opportunity to add to your vocabulary! To assist you, I have provided a glossary at the end. It contains definitions to standard words along with a few terms that I have fabricated as part of bringing Worm World to life.

Enjoy!

DJ Michaud

Chapter One
Separation

"Mom, wait up!" cried Wally. His mother's muscles tensed as she scooped with her head, pushing back dirt Wally's father was removing from the front of the tunnel. The tunnel rumbled, and fear began to pump through Wally's five hearts as he shook with the shifting earth.

"We can't slow down Wally," yelled his mother through a mouthful of loam. "The Diggers are right behind us. Get closer to me!"

The ground bucked and swayed as the tunnel squeezed in. Wally extended his body in a stretch and squeezed mucus from his skin so that his long, thin form would slide better through the narrow space. The ground shook again and the tunnel collapsed on his tail, pinning him. Wally thrashed in panic at the crushing pain. He caught his breath and remembered the escape steps from worm distress training – *scrunch* your front end, *wriggle* your middle to move the earth, *squirm* your back end, and *extend* your body. Wally stretched longer than he ever had. Each attempt moved him slightly, but the earth held him fast. He lost sight of his parents as they dug deeper

1

into the earth. Wally screamed the words as he performed the motions over and over – "Scrunch! Wriggle! Squirm! Extend!" In a desperate final pull Wally broke free. Panting through his pores, he launched himself down the tunnel towards his parents, dragging his smashed backside behind him. As he rounded the bend he spotted his mother, frantically sliding back down the tunnel in search of him.

Then the world around him slowed, and he saw everything down to the smallest details. A shiny, rusty wall dropped through the tunnel in front of him. His mother's face, frozen in shock, disappeared behind it. The wall sliced long and deep then pulled away, tearing the world in front of Wally with it.

"Mom! Dad!" shouted Wally. He squirmed forward and found himself high off the ground, half hanging from the side of a cliff. The shiny wall moved back and up, becoming a large, toothy bucket overflowing with the tunnel, the earth, the rocks... and his mother and father. Memories of their times together flashed through his mind – digging through rotted leaves, dancing in the warm summer rain, eating grass clippings. The cries of his parents faded as the bucket swiftly swung to the side and out of sight.

For one lonely moment Wally wished he could fly. If he had wings he could zoom up to that bucket and save his parents. It wasn't fair being a worm – forever tied to the earth, an unwilling victim of gravity. Why couldn't he have been born a butterfly or a flying ant? Then he never would have been caught in this situation.

The entire side of the cliff gave way, sliding and collapsing into the empty space below. Wally stretched and scrunched in the moist loam as the landslide dragged him along, terrified and alone. When the bulk of the ground stopped moving, Wally found himself half-buried, squinting into the harsh and unforgiving sun. Small rivers of dirt flowed past him, scritching and scratching their way down. Pebbles skipped along the surface, clacking into each other and shooting off in new directions. One noise rose above the din, a steady "bap-bap-bapping" that became louder and louder. Wally turned towards the noise and into the smooth stone that was bouncing down the landslide. "Bap, bap – bop."

Wally was delivered into darkness.

Chapter Two
The Bane of Us All

Wally rubbed himself awake, his head smarting as if the stone had hit him yesterday. But in reality, many days had passed and he now had little hope of seeing his parents again. The recurring nightmare of that day always left him wanting to squirm quickly to the surface and search for his parents, hoping they escaped the Digger bucket. Usually the Digger Day dream was followed by another, more fanciful dream. A dream in which Wally was a beautiful butterfly with shiny green wings, floating freely above the earth. A dream in which everything was right and nothing held him down. But that dream did not come this time, and the only pictures left in his mind were of shiny buckets and landslides, collapsing tunnels and bouncing rocks.

Digger Day had been traumatic for his entire village; thankfully most worms were not blessed with long memories. For Wally, the horrible dream that had at first come every night now came only when he was nervous, or anxious.

"Up and at 'em Wally," called Uncle Mort from the next chamber. "Let's take a good look at you, shall we?"

Wally squirmed into their living area, which contained morsels of rotted acorn, a slimy stack of sunflower seeds, and a few stalks of dying dandelions propped up against the wall. Uncle Mort checked him thoroughly. The landslide had squashed Wally's hind end, halfway to his band. Now his band was twice the size it should be – even on his better days he looked like he had swallowed a lima bean. The part that had been squashed was brown and coarse and hadn't grown along with the rest of him.

"Hmmm. Looks like you haven't been keeping up with your exercises young man," said Uncle Mort. "One hundred scrunches a day to build your backside muscles and twenty extensions to help slim that band. You are a Walk Watcher now, boy. That's a great responsibility."

Wally twirled himself around a dandelion carcass and munched the tender seed head in silence.

There was a time when Wally had dreamed of spending every day on the surface – exploring new places, facing new challenges, not being afraid of the light. Now he was done with daring and danger. He wanted to stay in his tunnel, safe in its deep, dank darkness. He heard Uncle Mort jabbering in the background but wasn't listening until Uncle Mort lightly leaned on Wally's damaged tail.

"You need a pick-me-up my boy. Walk Watching is the thing to erase your doldrums! Now, let's do a final run-through your training."

Uncle Mort had helped form the Walk Watchers shortly after Digger Day, and was its head trainer. "No member of my family is going to hit that sidewalk without being fully prepared!"

He fired through the Watcher checklist like a drill sergeant. Wally barely replied before the next question was blasted at him.

"What do you do with a panicked youngling?"

"Have them dampen their skin, open their pores, and breathe deeply."

"If you feel footsteps?"

"Spread out. Lay low. Make for the grass."

"A bird pounces?"

"Squirm down the emergency cracks."

Uncle Mort nodded. "And where are the emergency cracks on your sidewalk segment?"

"Square one, bottom right corner. Square two, across the center. Square three, at the root of the tree."

"Good job, boy. And remember, Wally, the Sun is NOT your friend. It is hot and dry and will cook you alive."

Yeah, yeah, Wally thought. *'When there is Sun, there's no time for fun. The day that is dry is the day you die.' Blah, blah, blah.* All these rules and sayings were meant to scare safety into the younglings, but Wally couldn't see how anything could be worse than Digger Day. The Sun didn't seem nearly as bad as that shiny bucket, or the tunnel caving in on him, or the landslide with the knock-out rock.

A short time later, Wally found himself in the ready room with the other Walk Watchers. They

7

guided their groups of younglings forward to hear the obligatory history lesson before being allowed to squirm to the surface to dance in the drops and sidewalk puddles. Wally had never sat through these as a youngling. There was no "sidewalk" back then, just a luscious lawn to squirm through on damp evenings and misty mornings.

A large, shriveled elder squirmed to the front as the group of groping younglings squirmed over each other in excitement. He spoke with drama in a vibrating voice. "Listen younglings, as I tell the story of The Great Divide, and how Lawnia came to be the last village left in Worm World!"

"Dampnia, Flowergarden, Ashland, Rockwall, Evergreen Hollow," the elder said slowly, pausing after each one. "All villages we remember with sadness and longing. All homes of our kin that were ripped from the earth on Digger Day."

The younglings let out a collective gasp of fright and stopped mid-squirm, transfixed by the elder's words. They were aware of the fact that their village, Lawnia, was alone in the world, but had never been told why.

Satisfied that he had their attention, the elder continued, this time varying the volume of his voice for effect.

"Before you were out of the egg, Worm World extended from our village of Lawnia, out across the fields and trees and stones and glades – all the way to the Barn. Beside the Barn was the most magical city ever known by worms... The Magnificent Mound! It

8

was the dampest, darkest, and most succulent of all places. Countless worms lived there and made their homes among the abundant organic matter. And it was a fast growing city! The humans showered it with new piles of food and bedding every day. Apple cores, grass clippings, flower cuttings, leaves, twigs. And peels. Oh, the plentiful peels! Banana peels, potato peels, orange peels – why there was even a day when a whole pineapple peel was added!"

But as easily as he had lifted the hearts of the young worms with his wondrous tale, he signaled a turn for the worse by making his voice low and throaty.

"Then one horrible bright shining day the earth started to move. Great gashes of topsoil were scraped away, taking thousands of our brothers and sisters, never to be seen again. Then, pile after pile of sharp gravel fell from the sky and spread where the topsoil used to be. The earth rumbled. The air became smoky and hard to breathe. So many of our kin were disappearing, that the Lawnia Village Council ordered all worms to the deep tunnels. There we remained for many days. When the rumbling finally stopped and we returned to the surface, everything had changed. Lost were the lush grass fields and the evergreen hedge. Torn away were the flower bed and the old fence. In their place, there was nothing. Nothing but the flat, black surface of The Great Divide!"

He looked quietly across the crowd, his head bobbing slowly as he scanned for the responses of the younglings. Most of them had balled up in fear but were listening attentively. He nodded.

"For many cycles brave worms from Lawnia would strike out into The Divide in an attempt to reach the other side, hoping to find the way to the Magnificent Mound. Only one returned alive... shredded, shriveled, and sullen. He babbled of the Sun and the stickiness until he went stiff from fright. Even the Wormy Corps of Engineers tried numerous times to tunnel below The Divide, but every time ran headlong into walls of impenetrable gravel."

He startled the younglings as he abruptly shifted his voice to a high note of happiness and encouragement. "But that is the past. So come back to the present – and the rain. The moist, cool, rejuvenating rain!"

As if on cue, the first drops of rain began to fall on the lawn above, resonating through the tunnel walls. They increased to a drumming pace, and the elder had to yell over the low roar.

"So when you go onto the sidewalk, have your first dance in the rain. Dance with abandon in the dampness of day."

"But remember to listen to your Walk Watcher," he warned. "They will be looking for birds and feet, sun and heat. And, most important of all, stay a safe distance from The Divide, the bane of us all!"

At his signal, the Walk Watchers' led the younglings up the exit tunnels and into the thick thudding drops of the summer thundershower.

Chapter Three
Tipping Point

Wally had argued when Uncle Mort gave him only three younglings instead of the usual five. But now on the sidewalk, he was glad he didn't have two more.

"Slider, stay close!" Wally yelled as the fastest of his bunch squirmed away over the slick sidewalk. Munch, a short fat worm, and his sister, Glide, watched and giggled.

Wally released air through his skin in an exasperated "hmmpf." He moved in his fastest awkward, half-abled squirm to catch Slider. "You two stay with me please," he instructed Munch and Glide.

Plump rain drops landed all around them, the larger drops making a deep resonating sound, the smaller ones giving off a high, clean tone. The various sized drops in between delivered a broad range of music to their ears. The clouds made the sky nearly as dark as night, and thunder rumbled and grumbled in the background as the air quivered. The overall effect was sublime – soothing and exciting, rhythmic and pulsating. Wally felt his midsection swaying, and the rest of his body followed. He had danced in the rain before and knew the hypnotic effect it could have, but he had never been in a thundershower like this. All of the sounds and sights and feelings aligned to produce a song that pulled the worms into a trance.

Even Munch was squirming his body, arching in time with the booming thunderclaps. Glide danced with Wally, who barely noticed that his backside had trouble keeping up with the rest of his body, or how his band would knock him off balance. Wally forgot about pursuing Slider and let himself experience the moment, welcoming the splashes of rain on his face and enjoying the thin coat of water that allowed him to slip and wriggle across the normally rough sidewalk.

This is heavenly, thought Wally. He lost sight of Munch and Glide as he was mesmerized by swirling clouds and the feeling of water running over his skin. For a few moments he forgot all of his troubles. But in the back of his mind he knew that this was the dance talking. Or was it? Could he ever be normal like other worms?

The raindrops slowed, and Wally's Watcher training kicked in. He stopped his dance and became aware of his surroundings. Not having the discipline instilled from the training, Munch and Glide continued their dance as they swirled and jiggled, trying to find the last of the larger raindrops that sloshed from the sky.

Good, they are both fine, Wally thought. He scanned the horizon for signs of the Sun, grateful to see only beautiful clouds and a steamy mist rising from the concrete. The beat of the dance still rang in his body and he squirmed with it as he continued to watch for the Sun. But something was strange with the beat. *It should be slowing*, thought Wally, *but it isn't*. And it has a funny bounce in it, sort of like a ...boing!

His body stiffened. *That's not the beat of the rain, that's a bird hopping on the sidewalk!*

"Ripper Robin, Ripper Robin!" yelled Wally. "All younglings to the cracks!" Wally squirmed to Munch and Glide and swatted wildly at them with his tough back end, trying to break them from their dance trance. Glide instantly became aware of what was happening and squirmed towards the nearest crack. Munch was a different story. He danced wildly and Wally struggled to immobilize him by wrapping his body around Munch's midsection.

"Wha, wha, what Wally?" whined Munch as Wally squeezed him so hard that their noses touched.

Wally screamed. "Ripper Robin, Munch! Speed squirm to that crack!"

Boing-Boing. Boing-Boing. As the robin bounced over the sidewalk squares, its shadow flitted back and forth across Wally and Munch. The robin's foot slammed next to them and rose again. Munch went straight with fear, then immediately curled into a shivering ball. Wally pressed hard on Munch's ball in an attempt to loosen him, but Munch was locked tight. Seeing the third escape crack a short distance away, Wally hooked the Munch-ball with his stiff back end and rolled Munch over the top of the crack.

Munch plopped inside and rolled to the edge of the sidewalk, then out of sight into the tall grass.

Wally squirmed into the crack himself, took a few deep breaths and tried to relax in the thin sheet of water that flowed into the crack from the concrete above.

I can't believe I lost myself in the dance and forgot about Glide and Munch, Wally thought. His stomach became tight and sour as he considered what might have happened if the robin had gotten them. But something didn't seem quite right. What was it?

Keep the younglings close.

At the first sign of trouble, stop their dance trance and head for the cracks.

Balled younglings roll well so don't fight them!

Make a final count – save all five!

Save all five? Well, it was a good thing that Wally had only three. Glide, Munch and...

Slider! Where was Slider? Oh, no, I totally forgot about Slider!

Wally rushed from the crack, ignoring the robin. He speed squirmed across the sidewalk, dragging his broken backside behind him.

"Slider, where are you? Slider, it's Wally, please answer me! Slider, stop your dance!"

Wally yelled over and over but heard no reply. Finally, he noticed Slider dancing wildly near the edge of the sidewalk, deep in his dance trance.

Boing-Boing. Boing-Boing. The bird hopped around the next sidewalk square, looking for its meal.

Please, please, Wally thought, *stay over there robin!* He squirmed with all his might to reach Slider before the robin noticed him. Wally was moving so fast when he reached Slider that they slammed together.

"Slider, wake up!" "Ripper Robin! Ripper Robin!"

Boing-Boing. Boing-Boing. The bird closed in on them.

"Oh, my," stuttered Slider as he became fully awake and looked past Wally. A faint shadow covered them.

Wally whispered to Slider. "Squirm fast. Go to the right. There is a small escape crack and tunnel there – just enough to hold you. Go!"

Wally pushed Slider to get him moving and found himself staring up at the robin's belly. He writhed in fear as the robin struck repeatedly, barely missing him and making an explosive "pock" sound each time.

First Mom and Dad, and now me, he thought as fear kept his body moving automatically. But from deep inside him came a surge of courage.

I don't want to die. I'm hurt, but not helpless. And I'm not bird food!

Wally remembered how hard he had struggled when the tunnel caved in. He wriggled and squiggled even harder now, every movement bringing him closer to the edge of the sidewalk. The robin pecked again, catching the hard part of his backside. It pulled its head upward so fast that it lost its grip on Wally, and he was flung into the air. Wally experienced something that very few worms ever had.

15

His entire body left the ground.

Wally spun higher and higher, head over hind end in twirling circles. His hearts pounded with fear and excitement. *I am flying!*

Losing sight of Wally, the dimwitted robin turned and hopped away. Wally fell back through the raindrops onto the very edge of the sidewalk. His backside landed on the concrete. The rest of him swayed wildly in the air as he tried to gain his balance.

Wally twisted. Wally turned. Wally tumbled over the edge.

And into The Great Divide.

Chapter Four
The Great Divide

"Ooh, ow, yeow, ouch!" Head-tail-head-tail, Wally bumped along a rough sloping wall until it leveled out in a flow of slow-moving water. He found himself in a concrete trough, bordered on one side by the towering concrete wall and on the other by a thick strip of black asphalt. The joy drained from him as he realized where he was, and he sloshed about frantically in the foamy water, looking for a way out.

Wally inspected the dimpled beige wall, looking up and down its length. Both the wall and the trough ran as far as he could see in either direction. Wally knew that this wall was the edge of the sidewalk, having once peeked over it during the euphoric and fearless period that followed a rain dance. He spun around to peer over the lip of the black asphalt. There was nothing – just a sea of flat, rough blackness sloping upward to the horizon.

Wally breathed rapidly through his skin, taking in what oxygen he could through the water rippling past. What was he going to do?

He curled into a tight ball and rocked himself, a trick his Mom had taught him as a youngling. By finding a happy thought and rocking with it, his fear would melt away, and his body would unwind. He focused on the feeling of flying. On having no parts of his body touch the ground. On the sense of weightlessness and freedom. And on the thought that, if he could fly, he would not need to drag his damaged tail along. As he slowly unwound from his ball, Wally realized he had a reason to live. A reason to fight on and find a way out of The Divide. He wanted to fly again!

With a new sense of purpose, Wally surveyed his surroundings. *Maybe I can squirm up that wall,* he thought as he noted how it curved up from the ground. He squirmed out of the water and extended himself up the steep slope in a rush.

This just might work, he thought as he moved quickly. *Keep at it. Keep squirming and pushing.* He felt the wall straightening underneath and made headway by driving his coarse backside into the rough concrete while stretching upwards with his head. But when the wall became vertical, Wally lost his grip on the concrete and toppled to the bottom. He tried a few more times, at one point seeing where the wall curved back the other way towards the sidewalk, but he continually fell back.

All worms believed that the sidewalk was never ending. Once a pair of daring worms had set out to prove everybody wrong, but they were never heard from again. And it was agreed that venturing into The Divide was so far beyond daring that it was most certainly deadly.

Well, thought Wally, *lost or dead is pretty much the same thing to me now. It's not as if one of my choices is to squirm down a tunnel home.* He laid in the gently flowing water and thought. Moisture was crucial to a worm's survival, but too much water caused a worm's skin to breathe poorly. Ultimately he would drown. And Wally knew that following this water would only lead to deeper and wider water. Then, sooner or later, to a river.

Probably not a good idea.

Wally lifted his front side over the lip of the black asphalt, using his bulbous band as balance. There was wet blackness in all directions. It didn't *look* too frightening. There was even a thin layer of oil on the top of the water, making it exceptionally easy for Wally to squirm.

Anything that makes it easier for me to squirm can't be all that bad, Wally thought. So with a mighty heave, he pulled his stiff backside up over the asphalt lip, and propelled himself into The Great Divide.

Chapter Five
Cooked

Rumbling, to a worm, is never a good thing. At best it means that rain is coming and water might rush into the tunnels. At worst it means something horrible is happening, like a big bucket digging up your parents.

Thunder had a similar feeling, but it made the air shake and only lasted a few seconds at a time. This rumbling had a humming sound that kept getting louder. Diggers made great tremors in the earth and made the ground shake from all directions. This sound was coming at him from farther up The Divide, but Wally couldn't see anything through the fog.

He turned to squirm back to the concrete trough, but it was gone. In every direction all he could see was black, oily asphalt covered by swirling mist. Wally speed squirmed away from the direction of the rumbling, extending his head in long thin pulls and then dragging his body up behind.

Suddenly a huge form hurtled towards him, floating high above the asphalt. On either side it rested on wide black stubs that rolled towards him along the tar. As the form closed on him, Wally saw it was a green monster with a wide silvery band across its front and a large bulbous eye on each side that shot light beams into The Divide. Wally struggled to move out of the light, but it was everywhere. Before he could move another stretch the monster was upon him.

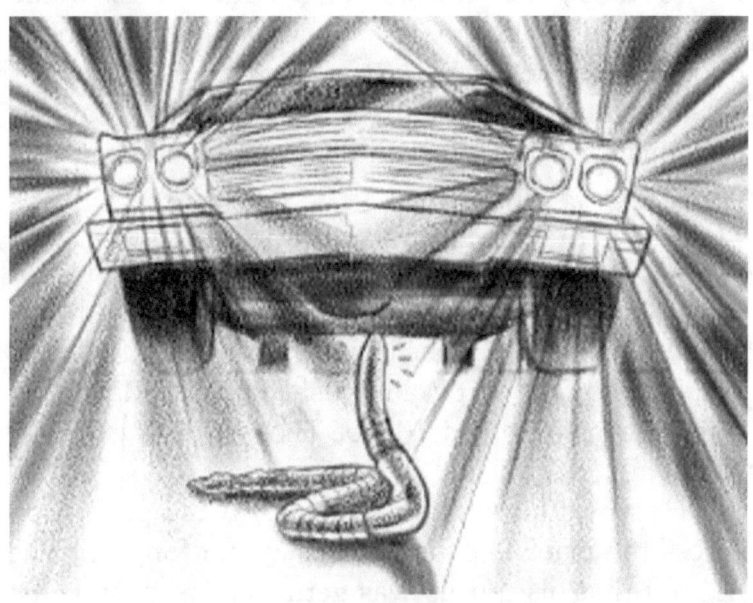

The black stubs were actually huge tires, and one was heading right for him. He had seen a bicycle drive past on the sidewalk once – and those tires had been scary – but this one was ten times as wide and much faster. It rolled past his head, squeezing oily water through its treads in jets that shot at Wally and pushed him aside in a foamy swirl. Wally was still spinning when another tire rolled past and spun him around again.

As quickly as the wheeled monster had rushed upon him, it was gone. Wally lay on the asphalt, breathing hard as the last of the water slipped past him. He thought of his breakfast nook and his half-rotted, half-finished breakfast. If only he could blink and be there, lazily munching and content. Wishing it would work, he tried blinking a few times. Blink. Grey clouds. Blink. Grey clouds. Blink. Sunshine. Blink – sunshine! *Oh no, not sunshine!*

Sunshine is the enemy of all worms. Every worm had this fact drummed into him from the time he oozed out of the egg.

But to Wally, the Sun's rays felt nice. They warmed his mucus, making it slimier and easier for Wally to squirm on the rough asphalt. He heard Uncle Mort's voice in the back of his mind. "If it's dry, you fry and die!" but Wally pushed ahead. Maybe the training was outdated. Maybe The Divide wasn't that bad at all.

Happy at his slippery progress, Wally pushed on across the black expanse. But it wasn't long until he noticed that his mucus was getting thicker, and that the thin layer of wetness on the asphalt was drying up. Soon Wally had to move from puddle to puddle to keep himself slippery and, no matter how much he moved, the Sun seemed to move with him.

"Stop staring at me Sun!" shouted Wally.

The Sun answered with shimmering hot rays. Wally imagined the shimmering was the Sun's way of laughing.

"You're not going to get me Sun," shouted Wally. "I survived a digger and a robin, so I can survive you!" But inside he wasn't so sure that this was true. One could get away from diggers and robins. But how could you get away from the Sun without being able to crawl underground?

Despite his discomfort, Wally pressed on. The puddles became paltry. Bits of sand clung to his body, making it miserable to move. Soon, small slivers of wood and tufts of fuzzy stuff were sticking to him. He twirled in a spiral to remove this gunk, but that made it worse. Sharp pieces of sand cut into his skin.

Unable to squirm anymore, Wally rolled and twisted on the ground, searching for another puddle. He became frantic as the moisture evaporated from his body. His backside hurt, his skin burned, and the beating Sun was blinding.

Uncle Mort's warnings rang in his head. "Run from the Sun. Your best bet is to stay wet. When there's no thunder, tunnel under…"

Okay, Uncle, thought Wally. *You were right. But I can't do any of those things in The Divide. There is nowhere to go, nowhere to hide. If I stay exposed much longer, all of me will look like my backside, dark and shriveled.* Wally lost the energy to twist and went limp, his gnarly hind end tipping slightly into the air. His heavy head drooped, his parched mouth hung, and his seared skin stung.

Wally slipped into a dream. Not a full dream, like hearing a good story that builds to a satisfying end. Instead, it consisted of broken bits in which Wally was some other creature. First he was an egg, waiting to hatch. Then he was a caterpillar, with many feet and suction-cupped toes. Then he was bound tightly and hung upside down, unable to move or speak. Finally, he was falling, with air rushing by. The falling felt fabulous! It felt like…flying!

Wally awoke to the sizzling Sun. It shimmered in silence. "Oh, you are a cruel, mean Sun," moaned Wally as he slumped over and lay cooking on the hot, black tar.

Chapter Six
B'next to Me

Wally felt the Sun prodding him. Then it rolled him over and dragged him along the dry, rough asphalt. All he could see was a rippling haze. Every part of him hurt. He wanted to scream at the Sun, but he fell back into blackness. Bits of light sparkled in the darkness as he was jostled around. Time blurred.

Wally awoke to his skin breathing in deeply, surrounded by a cool, pressing dark dampness. He coiled and extended, then swirled around to let the moisture flood his skin and become cool slimy mucous.

"Is this heaven?" he croaked through brittle lips.

"Well, not unless heaven comes in the form of a fresh leaf, lad." The deep, gravelly voice startled Wally, and he squirmed around to see who was speaking.

There was nothing but the green, waxy surface of a maple leaf that was folded around him.

"Who, who said that?" asked Wally.

Shadows moved and the leaf was gently peeled off Wally. A much larger leaf sat in the mist next to his. Underneath it, a large eye stared at him from the darkness. The being beneath the second leaf flipped its large tail and knocked the leaf away.

Coiled in the soft moonlight was the largest salamander Wally had ever seen. Well, he had never actually seen a salamander, but he had heard about them in stories. He had not dreamed they could be this big! The immense amphibian stood to face him, its long, flat head curled to one side so that Wally was staring directly into its right eye. Its two front legs were large and muscular, with one foot missing two toes and the other knee having a dimple where once was a piece of flesh. As it approached him, Wally could see large bright yellow spots on its glossy lavender skin. It blinked its eye slowly, its tongue sliding between stiff waxen lips. Wally noticed a large scar that ran across its head, through the corner of its left eye, and into its lower jaw. However, what should have been an altogether frightful appearance was softened by a playful twinkle in the creature's eyes.

"You, lad, were almost a goner," it said. "This is no place for a worm to be without wetness, especially one with a codgered up bicker like yours."

Wally was upset at this comment about his damaged backside and squirmed into a tight corkscrew.

"Aw, don't budger down lad, I meant no offense to yer. My name is Commander Alexander, Salamander," he said in a formal tone, bowing slightly. "Leader of the 12th Guard. Protector of the Sacred Log. Killer of Moggert the Mole. At your service."

Wally blinked, wondering where he was and how he got there. The last thing he remembered was struggling in the Sun.

The Commander chuckled. "You look much better lad. Good thing I scuttled up to you when I did. A while longer in that sun and I would be scraping you up with a stick! Lucky for us I found these leaves in a nearby puddle and was able to pitch a pup."

Wally could see the Commander's outline against the moon-lit horizon. He was easily ten times Wally's size, without counting the scratched and scarred tail that coiled back along his side and out of sight under his belly.

"Why did you save me?" asked Wally. As a youngling, he had heard tales of salamanders eating small worms.

The Commander winked his bad eye at Wally, the scar causing his lip to pull into a quirky smile. "I have never seen a worm so far into the road, lad," he started. "T'would not be fair to allow a being with so much fortitude to be shriveled by the sun." At this statement Wally's hearts were lifted. He did not know what "fortitude" was, but he was sure that having it was an unusual thing.

The Commander continued. "Plus I owe a great debt to one of your own kind, so it seemed the decent thing to do." The Commander hunched his shoulders, swaying back and forth rhythmically, his eyes looking through Wally, as if to some distant memory.

"What do you mean by a debt?" asked Wally.

"Scootle up here b'next to me lad," the Commander directed. "That's a tale that must be told eye to eye, for it involves the most majestic mate I ever had, and his part in our quest to save The Farm."

"The Farm" sounded exotic to Wally, and he knew that a "quest" involved daring and danger. Plus, the Commander's strong tone and twinkling eye heightened his interest. He squirmed over to the Commander and coiled into a small pile, as he had done when listening to bedtime stories as a youngling.

The Commander cleared his throat, shuffled his long body into a comfortable position, and began his story.

"In the age before The Road, what you worms call The Divide, everything around was part of The Farm. Creatures of all types lived in harmony in the fields and forests and glades. But a mess of moles sought to take over this beautiful place. To fight these hooligans, a grand army was raised from all the animals of the land. I led this army, and a member of your kind was my trusted companion. He saved my life too."

At this a small tear formed and rolled down the scar under the Commander's eye.

"Let me tell you about Farfetcher, the grandest worm I ever knew."

Chapter Seven
FarFetcher

The Commander took a deep breath and looked away from Wally, his eyes glistening gold in the moonlight. He continued his story.

"The moment you met him it was clear that FarFetcher wasn't your ordinary night crawler. He didn't run from danger, he ran towards it. A'feared of nothing that bucker was. He wasn't long like most of his kind; he was thick around and strong, and he could move like lighting. Fastest member of the armless race there ever was. And he could tunnel …even faster than a mole."

"FarFetcher was the key to communications within our army. He was my personal messenger, and would take on the most dangerous and important of communications between our legions. He could cover more distance in an hour tunneling underground than a cricket could hop on the surface. And he always came back with incredible stories that made even the scuttle bugs laugh!" The Commander lifted his head, staring into the night at far away memories.

"We had lost a big grappling with the mole army that day, and they had pushed us into the reedy marsh b'next to the stream. Moles hate water, so we knew they wouldn't bother us that night. We regrouped and prepared to push on them the next day, hoping the Toad Brigade from the Wood Pile would reinforce us in the morning. I had sent FarFetcher to bring battle plans to Gloap, the Toad King. Sleep came hard, so I took a walk through the reed forest, running our battle strategy through my head.

"Moles are a tricky, devious lot," he continued. "They are not particularly smart, and they are so blind they can't see their own front paws. But they can tunnel in the earth like a fish swims in water and their claws can cut you in half in a flash. Worst of all, they are notoriously unpredictable.

"As I stood amongst the reeds a bat swooped down from the sky and scooped me up like a newt just out of my egg," he said as he shook his head. "Should have seen it coming," he mumbled. "An alliance between the moles and the bats. An army of blind furry beasts that covered both land and air.

"The bat flew straight across the old soybean field and dropped me into the claws of Moggert, the Molemaster of the mole empire, and my sworn enemy. I feared he was going to eat me on the spot, but moles are a mean lot. He decided getting eaten would be too easy an exit from this world.

"It was late fall and the temperature dropped quickly as the night wore on. 'Salamander,' Moggert hissed, 'I'm going to make you an offer. Turn over your army and we'll eat only every other one of you.' I was so incensed by his cruelty that I shot my tongue out at him, smacking him right on his sensitive pink nose. He paid me back with a swipe of his claw, giving me this."

The Commander tilted his head so Wally could get a full look at the scar covering his eye. It was wide and long, and had healed as a soft purple that contrasted with his darker skin. Wally shuddered at what it must have looked like as a fresh wound. The Commander continued.

"The blow knocked me out, and when I awoke I was at the top of the rock wall. They had hung me over one stone, and pinned my tail between two others." He slid the end of his tail out from beneath his belly, and Wally could see that the entire end of it was flattened and scarred. The Commander nodded and looked at Wally with his good eye.

"That's another reason I felt a kin with yer, bucko. Beings with codgered up bickers need to stick together, eh?

"Well," he continued as the sky began to brighten over his shoulder, "back to my story.

"Moggert stood below me, and in his violent voice he screeched out to my army across the soybean field.

"'We have your Commander. Look how he hangs, helpless in the night air. When the hard frost comes he will slowly freeze. First his toes, then his skin, then his tail and eyes. Finally the cold will

31

penetrate him through and through and there will be nothing left but his cold, stiff corpse. And then I will eat his frozen heart!'

"He laughed across the field, and dared my army to come rescue me – suicide across the open field under a hoard of hungry bats."

Wally sat in silence as he listened to this surreal story of a time before he was born. Moles and bats, enemies and battles. He had never heard of such things in Lawnia.

The Commander's eyes rolled back as he gulped some air and prepared to continue.

"Bats are like moles with wings. Blind buggers who come out of nowhere and scoop you off the nice firm earth into the air – a place no well-grounded animal was ever meant to be." Wally felt conflicted at this statement. Instead of feeling sympathy for the animal getting pulled into the sky, he was jealous that they got to fly! He wondered why others didn't feel this way.

"These bats were known to lift their victims high into the air and drop them, then fly in spirals around the poor sods as they fell, laughing and teasing about what felt worse, the fear of falling or the pain of splatting on the ground. Without reinforcements, my army had to stay in the marsh and hunker down. Bats don't see like we do, but instead use sound echoes to navigate. The only way to beat bats is to mucker up this sound. That's what the toads are best at. Their croaks are just the trick to stop an army of bats. They were my only hope – but unknown to me, the toads wouldn't be getting there in time.

"You see, later I learned that FarFetcher had returned from his meeting with Gload, with news that the Toad Army would arrive at dawn. There I was at the other end of the field, hanging helpless on the rock wall with Moggert and his army spread all around. I could feel the frost beginning to form on my face. I thought I was a goner. But not FarFetcher. Because he traveled underground like the moles. And he knew a mole army that big had to leave oodles of tunnels under the ground when they moved. FarFetcher tunneled across the entire soybean field and under the rock wall. The ground beneath the rock wall was filled with mole tunnels, and since all the moles were on the surface watching me suffer, none of them saw him." A single tear ran down from the Commander's good eye.

"FarFetcher squirmed through the mole tunnels to the inside of the rock wall, and then squirmed straight up over the rocks until there he was, right b'next to me. He squirmed up to my ear and told me of his plan, warning me to be ready to jump when the chaos started. How he ever arrived at it I'll never know, but he created the most brilliant of battle plans." Wally listened intently, inspecting the Commander's face as the sky behind him grew lighter in the early morning.

"FarFetcher, by himself, tunneled from the rock wall directly into the side of the stream. The water from the stream shot through his tunnel and then

33

blasted into the maze of mole tunnels under the rock wall. As the water filled the tunnels it turned everything under the rock wall into a muddy soup. The base of the rock wall sunk quickly into this mud, and the stack of rocks shifted and slid, rolling down on top of the mole army below. The rock holding my tail rolled off too, and I tumbled to the ground, the wall falling all around me. Half of the mole army was crushed, the other half scattered across the field. Moggert escaped with a small band of his lackeys. We chased them down for many a day and finally caught them." The Commander cleared his throat and breathed in deeply. "But that is another story lad."

"What happened to FarFetcher?" asked Wally. He desperately wanted to know more about this hero amongst worms.

"Well now lad." said the Commander slowly, as the morning sun highlighted Wally's face. "FarFetcher was not quite so lucky. When the water rushed into the tunnels it took him with it. He was trapped in those tunnels when the stone wall collapsed. He was a true hero, sacrificing himself for a friend."

The Commander thrust his chin into the sky as a salute to his long lost companion. Immediately, the sunshine was blotted out as a dark shadow fell over him. For a moment the Commander' chin moved in small circles.

Then his eyes glassed over, and from the flap of skin at his throat came a gravelly hum.

Chapter Eight
Flight! (Sight!)

Wally watched the Commander hum and stare and bob his chin.

I have heard of this before, thought Wally. *Where did I... That's it! In Walker training. The "shadow stare!"*

It was a phenomenon rarely seen by wormkind because it required full sunlight (something worms avoided at all costs) and a large black bird called a Crow. The Crow would blot out the sun with its wings and flutter them lightly to make its shadow shiver. The poor unsuspecting creature caught in this hypnotizing shadow would fall into a trance.

"Commander!" shouted Wally. The Commander stood like a statue, except for his circling chin.

"It's a Crow. Snap out of it! Move! Run!" Wally felt surprisingly calm as he said this, and he mouthed a silent "Thank You" to Uncle Mort under his breath as he realized that his Walker training had kicked in automatically. Wally pushed all his weight at the Commander's shoulder, taking care to look away from the Crow and its shifting shadow.

Wally's efforts had no effect, and he realized he had to do something drastic. Wally pulled back his own head and thrust forward in time with the Commander's bobbing, striking the Commander directly in his scarred eye.

"Yeowtch!" yelled the Commander as he stopped his head and stared at Wally. "Why did you bop my eye when I was a thinkin' happy thoughts?" He glowered down at Wally with his scarred scowl. But then his irritated eye opened wide with understanding. The shadow on the ground around them was now half its original size and still shrinking rapidly. This meant only one thing – the Crow was diving at them. Or, more precisely, at Wally. Wally could hear the Crow talking to itself as it flew at him.

"Mmm, wormbly squirmbly for my chickies. Just the right size, goes down in one try!"

The Crow scooped Wally off the ground with its beak, its greasy black form skimming the ground before it swooped back into the air.

Wally's body writhed in convulsions as he instinctively struggled to free himself from the ebony bird. It was hard to keep fearful thoughts out of his head.

I'm gonna die. I'm gonna die. Why oh why do I have to die?

Wally fought his fear, reaching for courage within himself. A small voice spoke to him from deep inside.

You might not die, if you just try – to fight this bird up in the sky.

Wally started to cry. But not his inside voice.

Toughen up, don't you dare cry. At least you finally got to fly!

36

At that Wally opened his eyes.

And he saw for the very first time.

In front of and above him he could see only sky, but below him, oh below him! Wally had spent his entire life looking up – there had never been more than dirt to see when looking down. But now he saw how wide and wonderful the world could be.

There were flowing fields of silvery green grass. These were cut neatly in two by a long, wide strip of black with thin white borders. The Great Divide!

Running parallel along one side of The Divide was a white band made of small squares. On the other side was a vast expanse of green composed of many types of plants. Some were arranged in neat rows, some boxed with small fences of wood and metal, and others sat in raised beds of earth contained by large wooden beams. At the other end of this field of plants strung a jumbled line of stacked stones. The Commander's rock wall! Running alongside the wall for a short stretch, and then back through the gigantic green fields and under the black swath of The Divide was a sparkling stream – thin and fast in some areas, and wide and slow in others. And at the end of the green fields, up a gently sloping hill, was an enormous white wooden box with a rusted red roof.

At the bottom of the big box was a large mound, layered with leaves and all manner of matter, sprouting weeds here and there. Wally stared so hard he forgot to breathe, and his body heaved when he tried to force oxygen through the entire length of his skin at once.

Wally was in awe at this wide new world – at how vast and deep it was, at the amazing array of colors, at the way the wind blew past him and made the leaves shudder.

"Wormy stop so movey in mommy's mouth!" The words boomed all around Wally as they rumbled from the Crow's craw and blew past him on wet, warm air.

"Mommy no want droppy yummy wormy. Chickies hungry."

Wally's fear was gone, replaced by the thrill of finally flying.

"Is the world always this beautiful?" he asked the Crow with wonder.

The Crow shook its head in surprise at hearing its food talk. "World always beautiful wormy. Full of shiny miney beautiful things to take and yummy ummy things to eat."

The Crow flew on, spreading its wings wide in the wind. Wally noticed he was able to move a little every time the Crow spoke, so he kept it talking.

"Why did you choose me Crow?" he asked, as he prepared to move more of his body from the Crow's beak when it spoke.

"Wormy make nice squiggly wiggly treat for mommy's chickies, mmm, mmm. A morsely mouthful, mmm, mmm."

Wally thought of Commander Alexander and felt a small amount of comfort knowing that he must have escaped.

"Why didn't you take the big shiny salamander instead of me?"

"Wormy meal a tasty treat without the feet! Small chickies no eat-um boneymanders, them choke chickies up bad, mmm, mmm."

While the Crow was speaking, Wally moved his body bit by bit. It helped that the Crow had clamped on to his toughened backside; Wally felt no pain and was able to shift his weight so that the rest of his body was hanging outside the Crow's beak, blowing wildly in the wind.

This motion angered the Crow.

"Floppy wormy, stoppy movey!" it grumbled.

Wally knew it wouldn't be long before he got to the Crow's nest and was dropped into a baby crow's gullet. He struggled mightily, squirming his body in countless contortions against the side of the Crow's head.

"Wormy makey mommy mad! Mommy eaty wormy if wormy no stop movey!"

Wally could see the Crow's beady eye staring down at him as he twisted in the thin air. He thought again of the Commander, and suddenly knew what to do.

"Stoppy wormy, mommy – awwk!"

Wally coiled his body and struck the Crow in the eye with his head. In pain, the Crow's eye slammed shut and its mouth flew open.

Wally fell from on high, into the open sky.

Chapter Nine
Bait

Wally saw his new world through a colorful kaleidoscope as his body tumbled from the Crow's grasp. Earth – sky – earth – sky – earth – sky…

"Owch!"

Leaf – branch – leaf – branch – leaf…

Earth – sky…

"Oomph!"

The air was forced out of Wally's skin as he landed hard on a patch of grass, flattening a bundle of blades. But all Wally could think about was that he had flown. Really, truly flown! Strangely, he was grateful to the Crow and he sat thinking about all he had seen as he caught his breath. *Falling simply isn't the same as flying,* he thought. *I have to fly again!* He lay on the ground, staring at the bright blue sky that broke through the bunches of leaves in the tree canopy above him. The sunny day didn't seem so frightening now.

Wally felt the earth vibrate then stop, vibrate then stop. Human footfalls. The human voices boomed through the air.

"My dad said that all of this land was in the development plan," said the scrawny red-headed boy with the backwards blue baseball cap and torn-edged jean shorts. He carried a fishing pole and a white plastic paint bucket in one hand while he opened and closed a rusty pocket knife with the other. "But Mr. Patterson stopped selling off land after the first phase subdivision was complete. His Patterson's Potting Soil must be making him a ton of money. My dad said he was almost bankrupt before he invented that stuff. Now he is like a rock star." He shrugged. "At least he allows us to fish in his stream. And I know where to get the best worms. Over in the huge compost pile behind his barn."

Wally didn't understand any of this. Human language was made of short, hard sounds that were nothing like the soft, low tones of worm words.

The skinny boy led the way up a small hill towards Wally and the tree. A young girl with dark curly hair dragged her feet beside him, carrying an ancient bamboo fishing pole.

"Randall," she called. "I don't want to hook the worms. You do that part. It's gross."

"Aw, Shawna, you're just a sissy."

To Wally's horror, he reached into the plastic tub, pulled out a struggling worm, and threw it at the girl. She jumped and shuddered, shouting words that Wally knew would be not nice in any language. The boy flashed a crooked smile and threw a few more. Then Wally heard the strangest thing. From inside the bucket came a chorus of worm shouts, all with a peculiar accent.

"Squirm mate! Be free!"

"Make for the grass, find a tunnel."

"Look out for birds."

"Don't let the humans grab you again, bloke!"

Randall reached for another worm as he came under the tree. Shawna started swinging her bamboo pole in wide arcs to keep the boy away as she collapsed to her knees and began to cry.

"Oh, alright," he said. "I'll stop. Don't cry. For gosh sake, I was just fooling with you. Here, help me pick up these worms."

He patted the girl gently on the shoulder as he secretly picked a worm out of her hair and dropped it back into the bucket. He went looking for the rest, shuffling his feet through the grass and stopping every so often to bend down and retrieve a worm.

Shawna stood up but remained a few feet away, looking hard at him. "You're a total jerk Randall Ebbs. No wonder none of the other kids want to play with you."

The boy went to his knees, raking his thin fingers through the grass. Every time he found a worm and dropped it into the bucket Wally heard the worms inside let out a loud "Awwww" and then "Welcome back mate!" It seemed their whole goal was to escape the bucket and, while they were happy to see each captured friend again, they all wanted freedom more.

One of the freed worms suddenly appeared in front of him, squirming fast through the grass.

"Squirm mate!" he said, panting through his puffing skin. "That bloke up their will have you on a fish hook if he gets you!" He sped past Wally, and all Wally could think of was that he had met another worm.

"Wait, friend! Who are you? Where are you from? Can you help me get home to Lawnia?"

The frightened worm stopped dead in his tracks. "Lawnia? Did you say Lawnia? Lawnia was destroyed during the Great Scraping. You've gone daft from fright mate. Just follow me, and hurry!" The worm speed squirmed away through thick green blades of grass, looking back to yell a final warning. "Squirm you fool worm, his thumbers are almost on you!"

"Eww, look at this one Shawna. His butt is all shriveled up – or is it his head?" Randall had come up behind Wally and caught Wally's backside between his thumb and forefinger. He lifted Wally into the light to get a better look. "I bet old Chumbucket will love him. It will be like eating worm jerky!" He tossed Wally into the bucket, threw his fishing pole over his shoulder and continued up the grassy hill. Shawna shook her head and followed, still dabbing at her eyes.

"Chumbucket, Chumbucket. That's all you talk about. Who ever heard of a bass as big as a basketball?"

"Oh, he's there alright. And this little gnarly worm is going to help me catch him. Chumbucket has been in this stream since my dad was a kid. I know he is lurking there, waiting for the right food." He bounced down the other side of the hill, swinging his arms, the bait bucket in one hand, the pole in the other, heading for the wide and deep part of the stream.

Wally found himself on a pile of the richest earth he had ever seen. It was dark and moist, soft and silky. Not at all like the sandy soil at Lawnia. He thrust his head in, inhaling the sweetness through his skin, then began to tunnel. Immediately he heard worm voices, lots of them, but they were a fearful jumble. "...the hook...I want to go home...fish bait...swallowed."

Wally tunneled further until he ran headlong into a tangled mass of scared worms. They were in a cluster ball, the classic defensive posture in which a number of worms secrete mucus and weave themselves together into a tightly knit bundle. The worms then move continuously from the inside of the ball to the outside of the ball so that each takes a turn at being in both the safest and the most exposed positions. This approach made it difficult for any single worm to be easily separated by a predator and turned the whole group into one heavy, slimy bunch. Few predators could separate a well-made cluster ball.

The bucket bounced back and forth as the impatient boy walked on.

A worm on the surface of the ball saw Wally approaching. "C'mon mate, squiggle in here before that human grabs you!"

Wally instinctively dove into the writhing, slimy cluster, timing his dive into the ball so that he moved in synch with the rest of the worms. Immediately there were problems.

"Ouch mate, watch that bicker!"

"Who pulled in a twig mates? That thing hurts!"

"You could put an eye out with that!"

Wally's front end moved through the cluster ball easily, but his damaged backend kept catching and scraping and poking the worms he passed, causing them to fall out of rhythm. In mere moments Wally had upset most of the worms in the ball, and the entire thing collapsed into a slippery pile of confusion. The worms panicked and scrambled to reform the ball. Except this time they purposefully kept Wally to the outside.

"Sorry mate, can't sacrifice the good of all for one worm, ya know."

"Cheerio, lad. Hide behind us if you like."

Wally fought his fear at being ostracized from the cluster ball. He had been in one only once before, when he and his parents joined a large group of worms gorging at a pumpkin. An opossum came upon them and the worms had formed a ball in the center of the pumpkin. Wally remembered how afraid he had been of the opossum and how being in the cluster ball with his parents had calmed him. He channeled that feeling and found that he began to relax.

All the worms in the bucket spoke with the same funny accent as the worm he had met in the grass. One stuck its head from the mass.

"What in the world happened to your bicker?"

"Well," Wally replied, "I had my backside crushed by falling earth when I was a youngling. It's not so bad now. Sorry if I hurt any of you with it."

"Mate," replied one of the worms as he surfaced to the outside of the ball, "you sure have a crazy accent. Like you aren't even from Worm World at all."

"I was thinking the same thing about all of you!" said Wally. "Nobody from Lawnia speaks like that."

The worms replied in a startled chorus. "Lawnia?" And the writhing in the cluster ball sped up, as they all tried to get to the outside to see Wally.

Each worm would get in a few words before having to give way to the next.

"You've been to Lawnia?"

"That's just a story."

"There's no more Lawnia."

"The Diggers got it."

"There is nothing but road now, mate."

"So where are you from, really?"

Wally was scrambling to follow the ever changing faces that were trying to speak to him. "No, seriously, I am from Lawnia. The Great Divide separated Lawnia from the rest of Worm World. I crossed it to get here. Now I'm trying to get back home."

"Well, mate, then you have come to the wrong place."

"No back home for any of us, bloke."

"No Magnificent Mound."

"No table scraps."

"No orange peels."

"No mum and dad."

"We are fish food."

Wally couldn't believe what he was hearing. The Magnificent Mound? Orange peels? Could it be that these worms were actually from the home of all worms? He couldn't contain himself.

"Listen. My name is Wally. I *am* from Lawnia! Just like you all are from the Magnificent Mound! What I call The Great Divide, you call the Road."

The worms did not get a chance to reply. The bucket was dropped to the ground with a thump and the cluster ball collapsed underneath Wally into a wiggling lump of tangled worms. Wally wound up on top, his damaged backside sticking straight into the air.

A human hand reached in, shuffled around in the earth, and lifted Wally out.

Chapter Ten
Chum

"Hey, that's cool!" said Randall, tipping the worm bucket in Shawna's direction. "The gnarly worm stayed right on top, as if I he wants me to use him first."

"Okay then," he said, eying Wally with a harsh stare. "You get to be first pal." Randall threw himself into a seated position with the bait bucket between his legs, his fishing pole to one side.

The boy grabbed Wally by his hind end and lifted him into the sun, squinting as he inspected him. "How am I supposed to hook this bugger? I want to make sure he is wiggling well for old Chumbucket." He turned Wally over a few times, rolling him between his fingers while searching for the best place to insert the hook.

Wally was terrified. He had been taught to stay away from humans, but not because they would eat him! Yet, it seemed that this human was eying him with a hungry look. He squirmed with all his might, hoping the human might think he was too wriggly to eat.

"Oh yeah, look at him fight! Chumbucket is going to love him." Randall shifted his grip from Wally's stiff back end to his wiggling head and torso. Every time Shawna tried to turn away, he shuffled over so that he stayed right in front of her. "I don't want to hurt this guy too much." he said with a mean grin, holding Wally so that Shawna was forced to see. "I want him to fight."

Wally watched in horror as the human boy drew a fine, clear line from the tip of his pole. Tied to the end of the line was a wicked looking piece of bent metal, with a sharp barbed hook at one end and small backwards-facing spikes running up its shaft. Whatever the boy was going to do with that thing, it wasn't good. Wally tried to stay calm, even as he ran through all of his best escape moves in his mind, performing each one with his body in a constantly changing string of wriggles.

"Man, this feller doesn't want to be my bait today!" said Randall. "Sorry pal, you are chum for old Chumbucket. Just open up and say "ah" like a good little wormy!"

Randall turned his palm up, holding Wally tightly so that only his hardened backside stuck out. In his other hand Randall grasped the hook.

Wally hung upside down in the human boy's grasp and saw a flash from the hook as it moved through the blinding sunlight. He steeled his body for the horrible pain to follow. With a swift looping motion Randall pulled the hook through Wally's dried skin... but Wally felt nothing. To be exact, he could feel the tug on his skin as the boy set the hook. And he felt the weight of his body pulling on the hook. But he felt no pain.

Randall adjusted a metal clasp along the line. From his pocket he produced a round plastic orb which he attached to the line far above Wally's head.

Wally swung back and forth in great arcs as Randall rose then walked up and down the grassy banks of the stream, looking for the right place to cast. Shawna found a large flat rock in the sun and sat on her haunches, eating a white bread sandwich she pulled from her overalls.

"That's where Chumbucket is." Randall pointed with his fishing pole. "See, right there, in the calm pool next to that swirling water. He likes to sit still and snatch bits of food as they rush by." Randall found his spot and spread his legs wide, grinding his feet into the grass. Then he held Wally and the hook in his left hand as he made fake casting motions with the pole in his right. Up. Slightly to the left. A bit to the right. "Yup, that's the cast. I don't want to hit that willow tree on the other side and snag my line."

Randall let go of Wally and reeled in the line so that the plastic orb was just below the tip of the pole, Wally and the hook spinning not far below. With exaggerated movements he replanted his feet and balanced himself.

"Betchya going to snag it in the tree!" shouted Shawna. "That would serve you right too!"

Randall released the latch on the reel and held the line firmly with his finger. Then he leaned back as he swung the pole behind him in one fluid motion. His right arm thrust forward and the tip of the pole snapped straight as he released the line. Wally, the hook, and the plastic orb flew through the air, high above the water.

Wally was flying again, even if he was hooked to a line that was thrown from the boy's stick. He moved much faster than when the Crow had carried him, and the wind whistled as it rushed past. The top of the water was like the mica he had seen while tunneling near rocks, except that it was much clearer. Wally smiled as he saw his own reflection, and then stared in shock at the sight of the piece of metal entering his hind end and the barbed hook poking out of him. How would he ever get that thing out?

Behind his reflection he saw large shadows swimming under the surface of the water. They moved with a fascinating grace, undulating along. They had fins...and eyes... and giant mouths.

Worms didn't like things with big mouths.

Wally skipped once on top of the water and came to rest with a small splash. The weight of the hook pulled his backside down and forced his head momentarily above the water. He saw the boy, the blue sky, and a beautiful white flower with a bright orange center sitting atop a large lily pad.

And then he sank below the surface.

Chapter Eleven
Chumbucket

Wally's hearts beat out a rapid rhythm as the hook dragged him downward. He could stay under water for a short while – his skin trapped air that would let him breathe for a few minutes – until the water washed off his protective mucus. Then his skin would become water logged, and Wally would drown.

The line tightened. Wally's descent stopped with a light bounce and he was left spinning in small circles. He tried to think positive thoughts. In a way, he had flown again. Sure, it was at the end of a line, impaled by a piece of metal, but he had once again left the ground. And this time he had seen the world above the stream. How many worms had ever left the ground, let alone flown into the air not one, but three times?

But now the sky was far away. The cold water swirled around him as Wally spun on the hook. He could see the hazy sun high above him, its light piercing the murkiness and shooting off in all directions. Small floating particles glittered as the light passed through them, surrounding Wally with dancing shadows. To the side he could see no more than a few lengths before the water became dense and dark. And just beyond the border between the light and the darkness, shadows moved. In then out, in then out. Every time a little closer to the light.

Down below was blackness, with a large oval area that had its own, even darker, pattern. Wally's stomach tightened as he wondered what those shadows were, and what menace the dark oval presented.

For sure, floating was not flying.

Wally was in a bad situation. Under water, hooked to a long line that ran back to the human boy. He wondered. *Why would the boy tie a line to me and then throw me in the water? He must be planning to pull me back out.* That thought made him feel a little better. *But then, why throw me in at all?*

Wally looked down at the hook skewering his body. Suddenly it all made sense. Shadows under the water…worm on a hook…line to pull the hook back out…shadows with big mouths…big mouths that eat – worms! *I'm bait! I'm about to get eaten!*

Wally struggled to pull himself free of the hook. He pulled and pushed and wriggled and squirmed. He extended and contracted and twisted and turned. He caused quite a commotion with all of his motion. The shadows took notice. Then the shadows came.

First one darted out of the darkness. Then another. Then another, with each coming closer than the last. They had hard round mouths with sharp tiny teeth and heads that sloped up to spiked fins on their backs. On each side of their heads was a round, flat unblinking eye that seemed to look straight at Wally no matter where they were. They circled at the edge of his sight, shadows darting in the milky darkness. Their mumbling sounded like raindrops falling on dry ground.

"Mmmm, fish food. Worm food, mouthful, tummy full. Me first. No for you. Me first. Me do. No for you. Tummy full. Strike fast."

One came so close that it bumped him with its head. Another bumped him even harder. Then a third took a small piece of his backside in its mouth and tore it off in a twisting motion. Wally was horrified, but again felt no pain. Wally and the hook spun and swayed as fish after fish either bumped him or tried to bite him. He waited for the bite that would be on his fleshy part – and would definitely hurt.

"Mine!" The voice boomed out of the darkness, scattering the small darting fish back into the shadows. "My food! My dinner! My slopchops!"

A massive fish separated itself from the blackness and rushed at him. Its flat snout pushed the water in a wave that slammed Wally, causing the hook to spin wildly. When Wally slowed he was staring into a huge round eye whose pupil kept shrinking and expanding as it tried to focus on him.

The shadows hummed with a chorus of fearful voices from the smaller fish. "Chumbucket. Chumbucket. Chumbucket."

"Tiny worm-thing!" boomed the fearsome fish. "Human boy try to catch me with this shriveled snack? He needs to try harder, with something that fills me up!" He swam slowly past Wally, making sure to slap Wally and the hook with his tail in an overacted gesture.

Randall paced the bank, watching his bobber and peering into the water. "Hey, Shawna! The little fish didn't get my gnarly worm. Ooohh, there he is! Chumbucket! Look, he's circling my hook. Come on, big guy, bite! You want to eat that gnarly worm, don't you?"

Chumbucket circled Wally in a figure eight, moving in closer then swimming away, acting like he was going to strike at any minute. "I dislike human boy. Always try to catch me on hook. Always tricky with good food things to chomp. Humans catch my fish-mother. Humans eat fishes. Humans bad."

Wally half listened while trying to figure out how to escape. He could feel the mucus slowly dissolving from his skin. It wouldn't be long before he had no air left. If the fish didn't eat him, he would surely drown. Wally had no idea what to do, so he stalled by talking.

"Well, sir," he began. "If you do not like the boy, maybe I can help you." Just as he finished these words, the line pulled the hook in two quick jerks, causing Wally to bounce up and down.

"Ha!" replied the huge fish. "Little worm cannot help me! I am a big fish, but even I cannot stop human boy from pulling me out of water if I bite hook."

The immense fish gave Wally an idea. "What if you tie the hook to a rock?" He spoke this thought before he realized that it wouldn't help him to be tied to a rock at the bottom of the stream.

Chumbucket's eyes opened wide. "Worm nugget give me good thought. I am not big enough to beat human boy, but no human has ever caught Grandfather." He turned and spoke to the darkness. "Swirly fish, wake Grandfather and ask him to come." Chumbucket's command was immediately obeyed by the school of small fish circling in the shadows. They churned in a spiral that corkscrewed its way down into the black depths. Wally watched the strings of bubbles they left behind as they descended directly in front of the large, dark oval he had seen earlier.

He could hear the pattering voices of the small fish as they talked over each other. "Wormy hook. Boss hates human boy. Human boy afraid of Grandfather. Grandfather, please come!"

Wally trembled as he heard a rumbling voice reply in a tone that reminded him of the Diggers driving on the earth above his home. Then the dark oval separated itself from the blackness below and moved in slow, wide circles as it rose out of the depths. It was an immense animal – many times the size of Chumbucket – and Wally watched with amazement as it came near, staying below Chumbucket and outside of the light.

It had a large green and brown shell made up of hard plates in various shapes and sizes, all placed together in a repeating pattern. This shell was molded over its back like a tent, with a light-colored bottom forming the animal's hard, flat belly. In many spots the shell held scars and nicks that told stories of a series of struggles. On either side of its shell was a pair of leathery flippers, each ending in a row of sharp yellow claws. Its backside sprouted a stout green tail that it used as a rudder. Out of the other end came its head, square and hard, with a huge mouth that had a curved beak like a bird's. Its large, round eyes were placed under sagging eyelids that made it appear wise, yet slightly sad.

Wally stared at this strange creature for a few moments before he realized it was an old, mammoth version of the baby turtles he had once seen crossing the sidewalk back home.

Big bubbles escaped from its mouth as it spoke in a slow, purposeful way. "You send the minnows to request my presence. Do you not deem me important enough to come yourself? I should eat you where you swim!"

"No, Grandfather!" replied Chumbucket, as his powerful tail kept him well away from the turtle's mouth. "I stay near hook to make the human believe I will eat it. Many times humans have captured fish and turtle, and never have any of them returned. We both know their horrific fate."

Wally thought for a moment. *If fish catch worms to eat them, then humans must catch fish and turtles to ...eat them!*

Chumbucket spoke of Wally and the hook ignoring the fact that Wally was right beside him. "This wormfood has given me an idea." He mumbled something to one of the small fish, and the whole school swam swiftly to the water above Chumbucket and Grandfather, creating a stir so that Randall could no longer see into the water.

Then Chumbucket swam down to Grandfather so that his mouth was close to the turtle's flat, round ear.

"Listen closely, Grandfather."

Chapter Twelve
Pay Back

Randall couldn't believe what he was seeing. The little fish scattered and then Chumbucket rushed his line, but he wasn't biting. He seemed to be studying the worm. Randall gave the line a couple of quick tugs to motivate the fish.

"See Shawna, look at him! I told you Chumbucket was a huge fish! Any moment now he is going to bite my gnarly worm and I'll catch him!"

Shawna wiped her hands on her pants and strolled over. "Wow, he is big!" She thrust her hands into her pockets and stared at Randall with frowned eyes and pursed lips. "But you won't keep him if you catch him will you? I mean, seeing that he has been in this stream for so long, don't you want other kids to have a chance at him?"

"Nope." Randall eyed the water with a mean glare. "I aim to filet him and grill him up. My Dad will be proud of me for that!"

He continued to play with his line, trying to tempt Chumbucket into taking the bait. Suddenly the water erupted. The small fish were swimming and jumping, creating froth in the water.

"What? Where is Chumbucket?" Randall leaned over to get a better look.

Wally watched as the small fish swam in squiggly lines in all directions, and the water came alive with bubbles. He couldn't see or hear anything as Chumbucket and Grandfather discussed their plan. Wally imagined all of the horrible things that might happen. What if the huge fish ate him? What if Grandfather ate him? What if the human boy pulled him from the water and reset the hook through his good side? Thoughts of agony and death overwhelmed him. Wally struggled to free himself by wrapping his body around the hook's shaft and pulling away from his impaled backside. He had hoped the hook was not set too deeply, but his insides screamed with pain so he stopped trying. Exhausted, Wally hung from the hook and awaited his fate.

Through the cloudy swirls Wally suddenly saw Chumbucket and Grandfather nod in agreement. Chumbucket swam back to Wally as Grandfather moved silently in the shadows towards the shore. Chumbucket darted out of the shadows and seized Wally and the hook in his mouth – but the hook lay flat between his boney teeth and did not pierce the behemoth's lip. Wally's good side gyrated in the water as the fish turned and streaked away.

"He took it!" Randall whipped his pole back and up in an effort to set the hook. Chumbucket was pulled nearly out of the water, but he held his grip on the hook and played like he was snagged through the lip.

He mumbled to Wally as he swam. "You would make nice snack little worm, but this is more important. You will live to see our amazing plan…at least before the little fish devour you!"

Randall was walking up and down the shoreline, alternately pulling up the pole then reeling in a little slack as he let the tip of the pole fall. Shawna had gotten into the spirit and was walking beside him.

"But you have to let him go after you show …"

The shore exploded in a froth of water and weeds. Grandfather launched himself from the shallows and attacked the boy and girl. His mouth opened wide to reveal a wicked row of teeth, surrounding a lining of wet cottony flesh and a tongue of pure muscle. He hissed and spit at them, charging and snapping his jaws.

"Eeeeeeeeee!!!!" Shawna screamed from the depths of her lungs, spittle flying from her lips. She fell backwards, scrambled to her feet, and ran crying up the grassy knoll. Randall stumbled and fell to his knees, dropping his fishing pole. His eyes grew wide as he struggled to catch his breath. Grandfather lunged at him, snarling and snapping.

Chumbucket laughed so hard that he nearly swallowed Wally. He bobbed to the surface to watch the scene unfold.

"After he bites the human," said Chumbucket, "they all will steer clear of the stream!"

Randall scrambled backwards like a crab, searching behind him with his hands. In his frenzy he managed to turn over a large stone and lift it over his head. Grandfather sensed his fear and lunged for one of Randall's feet. Randall frantically heaved the rock at Grandfather, catching him square on the head. Stunned, Grandfather backed away. Randall found more rocks and kept throwing them at the surprised snapping turtle.

Seeing his plan failing, Chumbucket spit out Wally and the hook and sped away into the darkness. Wally's five hearts beat with confusion and fear as he sunk back into the water. What would happen now? The human boy would surely cast him back into the water to catch Chumbucket again, wouldn't he? Or, would he rip Wally from the hook and sacrifice another worm in his attempt to catch the big fish? Again Wally struggled to free himself from the hook. He pushed and pulled and wriggled and squirmed and felt his hardened backside begin to tear. Then he realized that his mucus was nearly gone, and his skin no longer absorbed air.

He was suffocating.

His mind filled with many thoughts. His mother and father. The Commander. Flying. Flying again, and again. The strange worms in the bucket. The mean human boy.

Randall found his breath again and, throwing rocks as quickly as he could find them, forced Grandfather to retreat back into the water. He laughed and screamed.

"Take that! And that! Heh, heh, heh! – Oh!" He tripped over his worm bucket and the foreign-sounding worms spilled on the ground. They began watching the scene curiously.

As Grandfather slipped beneath the water, Randall bent to pick up his pole. He began to reel in Wally and the hook.

Wally felt the hook jerk as it pulled him through the water towards the shore. He began to black out. *Ah, darkness*, he thought. *No more struggle. No more pain. Maybe I can rest here, just for a while.* As Wally slipped away, he had one last thought. *That human boy, he is so mean. Too bad Chumbucket's plan did not work.*

Wally was startled awake as the bumpy top of Grandfather's head brushed by. In that briefest of moments between thought and action, Wally became determined. He would not slip silently into the darkness. He would fight back! With the last of his strength, he twisted his body and spun the hook around so that the barbed end tipped down. Grandfather sped by and the barb dug deeply into the edge of his shell, dragging Wally and the fishing line along.

Wally struggled to stay awake as Grandfather, seeing what Wally had done, laughed deeply. Streams of bubbles enveloped them both. He spoke to Wally. "Fine effort young bait. What is your name?"

"Wally of Lawnia."

"This is for you, Wally of Lawnia." Grandfather dug deep with his flippers, diving down and pulling the line with a jerk.

Randall was yanked off of his feet and dragged into the stream. Unsure of what to do, he held fast to the pole and was pulled through mud and rocks, cattails and reeds.

Wally was barely aware of the chorus of laughs coming from the overturned bucket. In fact, he was barely aware of anything. He was drowning.

"Oh well," he heard himself say, "The world was just too much for me today."

Grandfather's voice boomed loudly through the rushing water and bubbles. "The world doesn't decide what happens to you, Wally of Lawnia. You decide what happens to you."

Wally realized what he had to do. In fact, he had known what he had to do all along. Other worms hurt their backsides and simply discarded them. Wally had kept his with him – the physical reminder of Digger Day and of losing his parents. But now, he had to move on.

With one big twist and the last of his energy, Wally tore free from his skewered self. Grandfather, the hook, and Wally's shriveled backside sped away into the darkness.

Wally was caught by the swirling current as he floated to the surface. The last things he saw were the overturned bucket on the bank and the human boy being dragged through the water, still holding his pole.

His oxygen gone, Wally slipped below the surface as his body washed down stream.

Chapter Thirteen
Sesquipedalian

Darkness. Swirling shadow. Mumbling voices.

"No hurt you wormy. We help'em wormy. Wormy get'em human boy. Wormy help little fishies. Save wormy. Save wormy."

Ripples of gentle nudges. Air, wonderful air. Beautiful, damp earth. Darkness. Darkness and comfort. Comfort and solitude.

Soft light. Shades of grey. Gentle mist. Five hearts beat.

Time passed.

Brightness and heat. Light and sun. Drying sun. Laughing Sun.

Talking Sun?

Why were you ever afraid of me? Sure, I can dry you out, but only if you let me. I am not your enemy. I help plants grow. I shine on the beauty of the world. I bring warmth and light and food. You and I are part of the cycle of life. We are friends.

In his hearts Wally knew these statements were true. That although some things were dangerous, it didn't mean they were to be feared. Just respected. He thought of all the dangers he had been through; of how many times he had survived. "I'm not afraid of you anymore!" he shouted. "I have been lost and saved. Captured and escaped. I have fallen. I have flown! I am bigger than my fears."

Wally rolled over in the bright silence. Every part of him was sore, but his skin was moist and breathing well. He looked up into the shimmering light.

"Am I dead?" he said aloud, as he stared up at a sky of clear blue.

"Well, if you truly survived all of those travails, then I surely hope not! I would hate to have you pass before we are properly introduced!" The voice poured from somewhere in a smooth drawl, startling Wally. He looked about and found himself lying near the stream in a shallow pool of shiny black mud.

"Then maybe I am alive," replied Wally as he searched for the voice's owner. "I don't feel dead."

"Fantastic!" the voice replied in a deep, energetic tone. "Welcome my persevering friend."

These words were spoken in such a warm manner that Wally immediately felt comfortable. He squirmed himself into an upright position and scanned the bank. At the edge of the mud puddle was a glossy black insect shell, overturned and rocking slightly on its center. Sunlight reflected from its polished surface in rainbows of streaked color. Along each side, sticking straight into the sky, were sets of long, spindly legs with hooked and gripped feet.

Wally wondered where this being's head was and squirmed to the other side of the shell.

His movement felt quite different. It was as if all his squirms before had been done while dragging a huge pebble behind him. With just a little push he could squirm quickly, and the spot where his damaged backside had been attached was already beginning to heal over, giving nothing but a dull pain. His band was almost normal size again.

On the opposite side of the shell Wally found the creature's flat wide head. It was made of the same smooth, hard shell and had bulbous, shimmering eyes on either side. Just below each of these eyes were short beaded antennae that continuously rolled up and down as if they were searching the air. It also had small, sharp mandibles below its mouth. These clacked together in three quick clicks as it rolled its eyes downward to see him. "Ah, greetings friend...earthworm," it said.

Wally was taken aback. "H-hello Mister, ah..."

"Juniper Alouicious Fieldcrest – June bug, aerial acrobat, and connoisseur of new experiences, at your service." He waved his front legs in what Wally believed would be a bow, had Juniper been standing upright. "If you are patient for a moment my new friend, I will greet you in the proper manner."

Juniper rolled his shell back and forth until he nearly flipped over. But he couldn't get himself righted. Great black wings slid out from between the halves of his shell and he beat these in a frenzied buzz that caused his shell to bounce slightly from the ground. He stopped for a moment; then again his wings hummed and throbbed as Juniper rocked his shell even harder. This time he merely managed to beat so much mud into his wings that when he stopped he couldn't get them fully folded inside his shell.

"I say, I would like to extend you a proper welcome, but I can't seem to right myself. Happens quite regularly, I must admit. Would you mind lending a hand..." He looked embarrassingly at Wally's lack of limbs. "Er, I mean assisting me?"

Wally squirmed to one side of the shell and rocked it back and forth with his head as he tried to right Juniper. On a few tries they got Juniper nearly up on one side, but each time the big shell lost its momentum and its weight pushed Wally back down.

"I fear I am much too big for you, sir," said Juniper. "But I am entirely to blame for my predicament. Fascinated with the world above, you know. I would much rather stare at the sky than look down at the gloomy ground. Flopping to my back is a cinch. The problem is, I haven't figured out how to flop back."

Flop! That gave Wally an idea. He wrapped his body around the shell near where it touched the ground and squirmed quickly, tightening his grip as he moved. His body became coiled like a spring.

POP! Juniper was pushed straight up in the air. Wally tipped him as he went up, and Juniper landed on his feet.

"I say! It is quite serendipitous that you happened by master worm." He spread his front legs and dipped his large head to touch the ground. "You have proven quite efficacious in freeing me from my quagmire."

Wally didn't understand all his words, but realized he was being thanked.

"And to whom am I addressing my heartfelt appreciation?"

"Oh, ah, Wally sir. Wally of Lawnia. Well, at least I *was* from Lawnia."

The immense insect walked gently around Wally. "Your claims of overcoming obstinate obstacles must be valid master worm; for I see you have recently shed your hind end. Only in the gravest of situations will a worm do that! I would love to hear an account of your journey. Surely, you are an heroic worm."

Wally felt embarrassed. "I'm not a hero. I am just a worm."

Juniper shook his head. "Ah, but master worm, it is not up to you to decide, but to those who hear your story. It is their role to sum your deeds and weigh them against what they believe a hero to be."

Wally had never heard anybody speak like this. In Lawnia there were no heroes, just everyday worms.

"What deeds?" asked Wally.

"What deeds indeed? Only you can tell them. Please, proceed with the tale of the journey that so fortuitously delivered you to me today."

Something about the comfortable sound of Juniper's voice reminded him of his father, so Wally relaxed and recounted how he came to be there, laying in the cool mud speaking with Juniper. He didn't leave out one detail, and as he spoke he realized how many challenges he had overcome. Digger Day. Losing his parents. Having a "codgered up bicker," as his new friend Commander Alexander called it. Saving Slider. The laughing Sun. The Crow. The mean boy. The hook. Grandfather and Chumbucket. Losing his backside. And flying! Three times he had flown, or nearly so. Frequently, Juniper would nod or add a witty comment such as "You fell over a precipice, into a precipice!" or "Oh my, fish food!"

Wally finished his story just as the Sun was fading over the horizon, slinking away as if it had been overshadowed by Wally's account.

"Bravo! That is an incredible tale my intrepid young friend. What deeds indeed!" Juniper clapped two pairs of his legs together in a clicking chorus. "You truly are a hero, Wally of Lawnia."

Wally didn't know what to say, other than a simple thank you. Juniper suggested that they make camp for the night in the safety of a pile of palm fronds. They scrambled onto the pile and feasted on some rotting leaves that had washed up from the stream.

"So, tell me about how you came to be here Juniper," asked Wally. "I'm sure you have an interesting tale too."

Juniper spun in circles, making a nest of the little leaf pieces around his feet. He lowered his head so that his eyes looked up at Wally.

"While you are prone to be prone, I prefer a supine view of the world, my earthbound friend!" Then he opened his wings, fluttered them in opposite directions, and flipped upside down again.

"The stars look splendid this way," he said with a wink. "Stars are empowering to me. They help me to think clearly. Remember clearly too."

He ran his right foot along each antenna, and then clicked his mandibles.

"My mamma was an Alabama June bug," he began.

Chapter Fourteen
Juniper's Journey

Juniper told his story at a deliberate pace. "She was a simple lady, but wanted more for her children than her humble home – a lone sorghum plant that grew in the corner of a dusty old hog pen. She wanted her children to see the world. Being gravid with seventy nine eggs swelling her abdomen, she couldn't fly. But she managed to hop a ride on a watermelon truck going north. To be honest, it had but a single watermelon in it. The biggest watermelon any bug had ever seen. In fact, it nearly filled the back of that flatbed truck."

Wally could only imagine how big that watermelon must have been. He pictured an enormous fruit the length of a sidewalk square and so tall that no worm could see its top.

Juniper continued. "The only other things in that truck were a bed of straw, a rusty tool box and a raggedy copy of Merriam Webster's New Abridged Collegiate Dictionary, Ninth Edition." Seeing Wally's confusion, Juniper explained.

"Tools are things that humans use to fix broken things. These tools were mostly metal and plastic –

much too hard and heavy to be of use to a June bug. But the dictionary proved to be the most amazing tool in the world. It was a repository of knowledge. A listing of words and their meanings. Food for the mind. In my case, food for my body also. But I am getting ahead of myself."

Wally leaned against Juniper and watched a shooting star cross the sky as he listened.

"Being at the end of her gestation, Mamma desperately needed to lay her eggs. Normally a June bug will deposit them in the rich soil beneath a large healthy plant. Her little larvae feed on the roots of that plant until they pupate. But the truck had a bed of stout wood, and the dry straw was no place for beetle grubs to grow. So she did the only thing she could. She laid those eggs inside the watermelon. Seventy-eight of them.

"All except for mine. I was a stubborn egg and wasn't ready to leave my mother's bosom. Mamma was so tired she crawled under the dictionary to rest. When finally I was ready to leave her, she could not find the energy to trudge back over to the watermelon. So, she did the next best thing and deposited my egg inside the pages of the dictionary. This small twist of fate set my destiny. In hindsight, it was the best gift a mother could give her grub."

Juniper turned away and rubbed his eyes before he continued. "You see, there was power in that dictionary. The power of knowledge. Knowledge delivered through the wonder of words – as many words as there are stars in the heavens. After hatching

I spent two weeks in that dictionary, consuming many pages. As it turns out, eating words is the best way to learn them. Mamma would read the words and the definitions on a page, and then I would eat through it. I plied through five hundred and fifty seven pages of Mr. Webster's book. Nearly twenty thousand wonderful words! I became the fattest grub my mother ever birthed. Seeing the defenseless state I was in, my dear mother used the last of her energy to guide me to the watermelon. I promptly ate my way through the bottom and joined my brothers and sisters, who were flush from two weeks of feasting on watermelon flesh."

Wally wondered what happened to Juniper's mother, but didn't ask. Instead, he let Juniper continue on with his story.

"Well Wally, that watermelon wasn't only the biggest fruit any insect had ever seen, it was also larger than most humans had ever encountered. The driver was taking the truck to the Great East Coast Fair, where the watermelon would compete against farmers' fruit from everywhere. On the last day of the fair it won the grand prize for largest melon – over three hundred pounds! My siblings were blissfully unaware of these circumstances at the time, since they were not educated grubs like I am. The entire time we were eating, I was listening to the humans speak to one another. I learned to understand the different sounds they make. Those sounds turned out to be words, just like the ones in the dictionary! They used words like 'superlative' and 'unbelievable', 'unparalleled' and 'tremendous.' And I knew them all!"

Juniper breathed deeply and continued. "But then we were separated from our dear mamma and her resting place under my wonderful Webster's. After it took the grand prize, the humans raffled off our watermelon home. The farmer who won drove it home in the bucket of a tractor to be the centerpiece for his summer picnic.

"You can imagine what seventy nine gross grubs eating away at the insides of a watermelon can do. When the humans sliced into our watery home they all moaned with disappointment as rotten rind, moldy melon, and fat white grubs tumbled out. Women and children ran screaming, one old lady fainted, and a pack of teenage boys rolled on the ground in laughter. Lucky for us, the kindly man didn't budge. He guffawed at the scene, shoveled all of us and the mushy melon back into the bucket of his tractor, and dumped that bucket on top of his compost pile."

"Juniper," interrupted Wally. "What is a compost pile?"

"Oh Wally, the heartiest home a group of grubs could ever want. Piles of organic materials that are layers and layers deep. Apple cores, corn stalks, grass clippings – nearly anything that humans have left over from their meals or from the workings of the farm. For us, it is literally a home made of food."

He smiled at Wally. "It is a habitat to countless worms as well. To be truthful, worms are responsible for its greatness. They learned to communicate with the farmer and decided to collaborate with him. The farmer would continue to pile food on the mound, and all he wanted in return was their castings. Can you believe it? He traded never-ending food for worm poop! The castings he used to create something called "potting soil" which he sold in clay containers to other humans.

These humans used the soil to grow flowers and food. Over time, the farmer experimented with all types of food, creating different variations of castings that helped certain types of plants to grow faster and stronger. As he progressed, the compost pile grew into such a perfect place to live that the worms thrived and built an entire city in it. It is a beautiful, marvelous, magical place.

"I'm surprised you haven't heard of our Magnificent Mound!"

Chapter Fifteen
Mound Around

Wally swallowed hard, not believing what he had heard. His words came out dry and slow. "Did you say The Magnificent Mound?"

"Why yes," answered Juniper. "In fact, all my siblings live there too. They are castings collectors, and jolly good at it, if I do say so myself. Even their grubs pitch in. Grubs are extremely efficient at digestive processing!"

Wally was dumbfounded. His skin whistled as his breathing sped up to keep pace with his rumbling hearts. He coiled up so that his head was lifted from the ground and looked into Juniper's upside-down eyes. "The Magnificent Mound," he said again, in a dreamy manner. "Are we near it? Can we reach it from here?"

Juniper thought for a moment, and a sad look crossed his face. "Unfortunately, you are terrestrial, my friend. For a June bug, flitting between one spot and another is a simple feat. But for earthworms, travelling long distances is not an option. Though, I must say, you seem to be an exception to that rule. What I mean, is that I can fly to the Mound with relative ease. But crawling there, well, it would take you quite a while to traverse the distance. And there are many dangers to a worm along the way. It is not impossible, but it is arduous."

Wally slunk into the wet ground, his head hung low. "I can't go home across The Great Divide. It nearly killed me. Without the Commander saving me and the Crow snatching me, I surely would have died from the Sun. But if I could get to the Magnificent Mound somehow..." He shrugged, his face scrunched together in determination. "If I need to crawl there, then that is what I'll do. I have to look forward now, not back."

He squirmed a short distance and looked back at Juniper. "It won't be easy. I could use a friend to help me along the way. Like you said, it will be a dangerous journey. And a lonely one."

Juniper cried. First in light gasps and then in large sobs that caused the shells covering his wings to open and close, spinning him in a slow circle. His antennae unrolled and his tears ran down them and onto the ground.

Embarrassed, Wally dug his nose into his side. "I'm sorry Juniper, I didn't mean to upset you, I just thought that..."

"Oh, no, no, no!" Juniper slowed his sobs and his shell spun to a stop, his head facing Wally. "Nobody ever asked me to be his friend before. June bugs with extensive vocabularies tend to be intimidating."

His antennae curled up as he wiped away the remaining tears with his front legs. "Master Wally, it would be an honor to travel with such a hero as you. To be your humble companion." He smiled. "If we are to travel by foot, or in your case by belly, then we should get a thorough rest. I don't suppose, before we do, that you might perform the service of flipping me right side up?"

Wally laughed. What a strange pair they were, yet how well they went together. He coiled himself around Juniper's shell and POP! Juniper was right side up. They lay under some rotting leaves and quickly fell asleep.

Snippets of dreams passed through Wally's mind. Crawling, falling, flying, almost dying. A lost backside. Juniper popping. Crawling. The laughing Sun. Crawling. Flying... but this time somehow being in control. Having no fear, the wind blowing against his skin with the world below and around him. The buzz of beating wings. In the background he heard Juniper talking in his sleep. He awoke to a clear, dark sky full of bright shining stars, an idea crystallizing in his mind.

"Juniper," cried Wally. "Wake up!"

Wally spoke excitedly as Juniper poked his head from beneath a soggy brown oak leaf.

"Juniper, I can't fly. But you can. And you are much bigger than I am. Do you think you could carry me?" Wally squirmed with anticipation, his head bobbing as he stared at Juniper. Juniper clacked his mandibles a few times in thought, rolling his antennae in and out.

"I don't see why not. My thrust to weight ratio is much more than I need. And I have carried food in flight before. You can't weigh more than half a birch leaf, especially with your missing backside." Juniper realized he had mentioned Wally's injury, and he stared at the ground, shifting dirt between his front legs.

Wally was far too excited to notice. "Can we try right now?" Without waiting, Wally squirmed onto Juniper, squeezing his body between Juniper's head and the point where his shell connected. Juniper shifted his wings a few times as Wally searched for the right position, finally settling with his head upright and his shortened backside coiled around Juniper's neck.

Juniper thrummed his wings into motion and did a series of short flights, bouncing firmly back to the ground each time to test Wally's grasp. Wally tipped his head next to Juniper's and yelled over the noise. "If you can carry me, I can hold on. Let's fly!"

"With all celerity, Master Wally!"

Juniper extended his wings in a full buzz and bounced into the air.

Chapter Sixteen
Airborne

Wally had flown through the air three times. But being thrown into the air by a Robin and being attached to a hook cast into the air were not *really* flying. Even though the Crow was flying, Wally had been a captive morsel – a piece of food for a nest of hungry chicks – with no control over where he was going.

Plying the sky with Juniper was flying at its best. He never flew in a straight line and rarely stayed level. Juniper would sway left, then right, then slow down, and then speed up. Every so often he would do a loop-de-loop and Wally would have to grip with his entire body to keep from rocketing off. Wally's skin tingled.

"Sorry about the random trajectories, Wally," shouted Juniper, "but one must never fly in a straight line you know. In daytime birds are always looking for a nice fat June bug, and at night the bats are just as treacherous. Add a juicy worm to the package and we make quite an enticing entrée! But if we keep moving, we will be fine."

Wally was thrilled. The cool night air on his skin brought a new scent every second – sweet and succulent sunflowers, a hint of salt from the nearby ocean marsh, the pasty bitterness of burning wood, and the nasty smell of freshness as they passed over a long line of human clothes hanging in the light breeze. That was the absolute worst! Worms liked everything half rotten and the smell of fresh and clean made Wally's stomach turn. The light of the nearly-full moon painted the land below and Wally was amazed at how wide the world was.

As Juniper spiraled higher into the sky, Wally could see the dark lines of the stream and the winding path of the Road. It went up and down a few small hills, split the Rock Wall, ran over the stream, into the Woods and then ended where it looped back upon itself. The buildings along each side of the Road were of different shapes and sizes, separated from each other by rows of manicured shrubs or small stone walls or white picket fences. In the distance Wally could see lights on another building that sat alone and, not far from it, a building that was so huge it could have fit any three of the other buildings inside. Alongside this building ran multiple squat, long buildings that reflected the moonlight in soft flashes.

"Juniper, is that the Farm? And is that big thing the Barn?" Wally shivered with excitement.

"Why, yes Wally. That is what is left of the Farm. Before the subdivision, all the land around us was part of the Farm. Now only a portion is left – the house, the Barn, the greenhouses, and the surrounding fields that the Farmer tills. The long rows of buildings that line the Road are the subdivision – all houses for human families."

The Road. The Great Divide. Wally's throat tightened as he thought of Digger Day, at the loss of so many villages, at the separation of Lawnia from the rest of Worm World, and at the memory of the bucket scooping his parents away. But this time he vowed to fight his fears. A chill determination gripped his hearts as he realized what he needed to do. "Juniper, can we fly over The Divide?"

Juniper nodded. "Why sure, Captain Wally!" he said proudly. "Juniper Airlines at your service."

Juniper dove in a long, slow arc along the stream, then over the rock wall and the fields, and leveled off above the tree line that separated them from The Divide. He followed the row of trees to its end, and dipped over The Divide at its loop-around. Wally squeezed hard, and Juniper buzzed in place for a few moments until he felt Wally loosen a bit. Then he flew slowly down the center of The Divide.

Wally was awash with emotions. Sadness, excitement, exhaustion. And anger. Anger that his parents were ripped from him, anger for the villages lost to The Divide, anger at his lost backside. And anger at himself, that he had allowed all of these things to haunt him for so long. His emotions screamed out of him as they flew.

"I am Wally of Lawnia. You squashed my backside, took my parents, and destroyed half of my village. But I am no longer afraid of you. You are just a Road. A thing made by humans. I am Wally. And this is Juniper. See us fly!!!"

Juniper swerved side to side, moving up and down as they zoomed the length of the tarmac. Wally surveyed the Road, observing its dips and turns, seeing the sidewalk and how its edge became the curb that rolled down to the Road. A car drove beneath them and Juniper took care to fly higher to avoid its airstream. All Wally's fears were beneath him now, and this new perspective brought him an inner strength and calmness. He no longer felt like yelling. After all, it was just a road with a car on it, separated from the human houses by a long sidewalk. Nothing to fear.

The road came to an abrupt end as it spilled into the side of another road. This new road seemingly ran forever in both directions. But to Wally's right it went in front of the Farmhouse and Barn...and Wally knew that near the Barn was the Magnificent Mound!

"Juniper, can we fly there? To the Magnificent Mound?"

Juniper did not reply.

"Hmmmmm..." Juniper's head swayed towards one of the human houses. He turned and dove rapidly. Wally was almost thrown off and he gripped Juniper with his entire torso as they went faster and faster.

"Juniper, what's the matter?" Wally yelled. "Is there a bat around?"

"Hmmmmmmmm..."

They were moving so fast that Wally could barely see through the wind rushing past his face. Juniper dove along the back of the first human house, towards a glowing blue light. As they approached, Wally could see the light came from four upright blue rods that were arranged in a circle. Surrounding them was a finely meshed metallic cage and the whole works was hanging from a post in the backyard.

The cool blue of this light welcomed and soothed Wally. It hummed and buzzed, and now and again a bright flash would appear with a zap and a crackle. Juniper began humming in tune and flying in a circle around the pole. Flush with his newfound strength and confidence, Wally broke one of the most important of worm rules and allowed himself to enjoy the light. Suddenly, a large mosquito flew past them and almost hit Wally with one of its wings. It, too, was humming in tune with the light and was completely unaware of anything around it.

More bugs appeared in the sky – lady bugs, mosquitoes, gnats...and moths. Hundreds of moths in all shapes and sizes flying in many directions. Some were hovering around the light. Others were flying in crazy loop-de-loops. Still others flew in wide jerky circles. Juniper joined this circus of flying bugs, humming with a blank stare. He, too, began moving in wild loops, in and out from the light. Suddenly Wally noticed a burning smell in the air, and his sense of fear returned.

A tiny black fly broke from its pattern and performed a buzzing dive straight into the light.

ZAP!

The mesh glowed hot and bright as the bug hit it. With a small puff of smoke the fly disappeared. The other bugs wavered for a moment, and then continued their crazed flying. As Juniper turned in to a tight loop, Wally noticed the ground below the light. It was littered with the bodies and shells of dead bugs. This light was a bug killer!

"Juniper! Fly away!"

But Wally's warning was too late. They were at the top of a long loop and, for a moment, they stopped – almost weightless in mid-air. Juniper dipped his shoulder and shot towards the light. Everything became a blue blur. Juniper hummed loudly and thrummed his wings, increasing their speed even more. Wally was thrown backwards, hanging on for his life. He screamed at Juniper.

"The light is a trap! It will kill us! Get away from it!" But Juniper did not listen. He hummed and flew so fast that his antennae were pushed flat across his head.

In desperation, Wally grabbed one of Juniper's antennae in his mouth and pulled with every muscle in his body. Juniper's head snapped to one side, and at the last moment his entire body turned. But it was too late.

Juniper's right wing covering struck the light.

BANG!

The flash blinded Wally and greasy smoke poured over his skin. Then they fell.

Chapter Seventeen
Bound for the Mound

Juniper beat his good left wing wildly. Wally held on for his life as Juniper's other wing fluttered and buzzed, its half-shell cover wobbling with wisps of smoke. They shuddered into a wide descending spiral. Juniper's eyes were glassy and confused.

"Juniper, are you okay?" Wally yelled above the commotion.

Juniper shook his head a few times and the glaze left his eyes.

"Master Wally," Juniper said with a slur, "What happened? The last thing I remember is that we were flying to the Magnificent Mound. Now I find myself injured and smoldering."

Wally explained, and as he got to the part where they went into the light, a bug above them slammed into the mesh with a POP. The poor thing dropped past them in a tangle of wings and long legs.

"Thank you for rescuing us from that entanglement," said Juniper. "The human in that house must be very cruel to put something so beautifully lethal in his yard!"

As they approached the ground, Wally avoided looking at the bits and pieces of zapped bugs littering the area below the light. It was tough being an insect, whether walking, crawling or flying.

Juniper regained control of his right wing and leveled off a few inches above the ground, carefully flying away from the light and the house. They gradually gained altitude, and Wally could once again see the Barn, with the long rows of greenhouses glittering in the moonlight beside it.

Juniper popped over a line of apple trees and flew along the Rock Wall, then turned directly towards the Barn, passing over the fields. Every time Wally tried to catch his eye, Juniper would look away. As a result they flew in silence, and Wally had time to think about where they were going.

All his life he had heard stories about the Magnificent Mound. The art and culture, the wide tunnels, the high halls. The lush layers of incredible edibles and perfectly cool dampness. And the many types of worms and other bugs that lived together in harmony. Wally imagined what each bug would look like.

The fields unfolded below them in endless rows of vegetables. First, long lines of corn. Then, stands of tomatoes. Mounds of cucumbers zoomed by beneath them, leading to stretches of green beans, peppers and cabbage. Peas, carrots, potatoes, broccoli – always something new after a few rows. Finally they neared the back wall of the Barn, and Wally could see a dark pile at its base. As they got closer, the pile began to take shape in the half light of the early dawn.

Juniper circled the Mound so that Wally could take it all in. The Mound was gigantic – even to humans it must have seemed quite large. But to worms and insects, it occupied an entire world of space. From one end to another it could have held many Lawnia's and still had room for all the other villages in Worm World. On top were piles of partially-rotten food and decomposing discards, each one different from the others. They were colored by peels and pieces from unknown fruits and vegetables. One pile consisted of curly brown slivers that looked to be carved from a root. One had the cores of a fruit with a woody stem and yet another bright green stalks that looked like small trees with some of their branches chewed off. Another had large peels with bumpy orange outsides and a soft white inside. The final one had shredded pieces of paper printed with letters and pictures. Juniper saw this one and mumbled something about not having eaten any new words in a while.

Ringing the sides of the Mound were larger piles made of yard clippings – grass, hedge, brush, leaves – all mulched into thick alternating layers. On the ground at the bottom of the Mound were a series of neat hills made entirely of worm castings. These hills were being formed by scores of June bugs who were scraping the castings from tunnels at the base of the Mound and sweeping them forward with their front legs. Wally saw that they did not always return to the same hill every time. One of the bugs scurried about calling out instructions to intermix castings from different tunnels. Beside her stood another June bug with huge front legs who would dive in and help push castings if any one of the other June bugs fell behind.

As the sun peaked over the horizon, they flew to the base of the Mound towards the large-legged June bug, who was even bigger than Juniper. He stared bug-eyed as Juniper and Wally landed with a bounce.

"Greetings my kin!" Juniper said with a bow. As he spoke, Wally slid onto the ground. "This is my new friend Wally, of Lawnia." Juniper waved his head to each of the June bugs as he introduced them to Wally. "And this is Cockleburr and Quidnunc, my brother and sister." They bobbed their heads to Wally, both staring with their mouths open.

"Very nice to meet you." Wally waved his hind end in a traditional worm greeting, noticing that his damaged backside was now nearly healed and a new tail stub had begun to grow. His five hearts jumped inside of him.

Quidnunc scrambled over to Juniper and rubbed antennae with him. "I am pleased to see you brother! We feared that you were somewhere stuck upside down." She grinned at Juniper and then winked at Wally. "I can only assume your new companion has helped you with this situation." Cockleburr scuttled up beside Quidnunc.

"Did my brother say Wally of *Lawnia*?" he asked in a raspy voice. "I thought Lawnia was destroyed during the days of the Great Scraping. Did you somehow escape?"

Juniper was so excited that he answered before Wally had a chance to speak.

"Brother, only part of Lawnia was taken. Wally endured the Great Scraping and has traveled here through terrible tribulations. He has suffered through sun and heat, survived the Robin and the Crow, and even crossed the Road itself! He is the first worm to fly through the air – in four different modes, I might add!" He paused for a moment. "Though I'm sure he enjoys June bug flight the best!"

Quidnunc's eyes opened wider as she listened to her brother's descriptions. "He even survived being placed on a hook by the human boy! Why, he outsmarted Chumbucket in his own domain. He is a worm above worms. He is a true hero."

Quidnunc's front feet came together forcefully. "On a hook you say?"

Juniper nodded.

"Chumbucket, the huge fish?" inquired Cockleburr.

Juniper nodded again.

"And you flew all the way here...together like that?" finished Quidnunc.

"Yes," said Wally and Juniper in unison.

Quidnunc looked at Wally in silence. Her eyes sparkled and she nodded her head a few times. Cockleburr clacked his mandibles together lightly in approval.

"Wally has had a long journey, and we are both tired and hungry," said Juniper. "Perhaps you might run ahead and prepare a place for us to rest our weary bodies and partake in some sustenance."

Quidnunc grinned at the opportunity. "Oh, yes Juniper. I would love too!"

Juniper leaned close to Wally and whispered. "She is an incorrigible gossip, but she has good intent. And you should see the plants that grow from her blendings!"

As Quidnunc scrambled off, Cockleburr bowed slowly to Wally. "I would be honored to guide you on a tour of our city, Master Wally," he said in a deep tone. "We shall start at the bottom, where our true livelihood lays."

He walked along the flat ground at the base of the Mound, weaving in and out of chocolate-colored piles of castings. Juniper followed as Wally listened closely to Cockleburr.

"Only a few generations ago, our Mound was not nearly so magnificent. It was a large pile made of old manure and earth, home to many worms but not the grand city it is today. Sometimes the humans threw yard clippings on it, but mostly the worms scavenged for food."

He spread his forelegs wide. "One day the humans placed the remains of a gigantic watermelon on top of the Mound. In that watermelon were my brothers and sisters and me, though we were newly hatched grubs. The worms adopted us, and together we feasted on the remains of the watermelon for many cycles. By the time it was finished we had made so many castings in the Mound that we had to pile them outside. The Farmer's daughter saw these piles and took them away. Soon she returned with a basket of old cabbages that had been rotting in the sun. We ate those too and created more castings. Again, she took the piles of castings away and deposited more fabulous food on the top of the mound."

Cockleburr tapped Juniper on the shoulder with one leg. "With Juniper's guidance, the worm elders learned how to communicate with the Farmer's daughter. Every worm knows that what we eat comes out our backside as castings. What we did not know was that these castings are especially nutritious for plants. With his daughter's help, the Farmer and the elders struck a deal. He would keep bringing more food and all we had to do was to give him our castings! Over time we learned that various foods create different types of castings and that particular types of plants prefer certain blends."

He stopped and waved an antenna to the piles they had been making when Wally and Juniper arrived. "June bugs like Quidnunc are called Blenders. They are responsible for knowing the recipes to mix multiple castings in different proportions. Quidnunc is the best Blender of all. She is constantly inventing new recipes for the Farmer to try." He held up his long forelegs. "Large June bugs like me are responsible for harvesting the castings for Blenders to use."

He turned towards the Mound. "But I am getting ahead of myself. You will learn everything about how our great city functions on your tour." He waved a foreleg towards the largest tunnel. "After you, Master Wally."

As they walked, Wally looked up at the Mound. It was a thousand times taller than he was and so wide that he could not see either end. What a magnificent sight it was!

Quidnunc must have told others in the Mound of their arrival, for an elder met them at the tunnel entrance. He looked far older than the oldest elder of Lawnia, and the darkness of his purple band showed that he was towards the end of a long life. He was wrapped in a robe made from bright colored strips of paper, and a crooked leaf was tied to his neck so that it tipped over the front of his head, almost like a crown. A worm who dressed! Wally knew he was in the presence of one of the original elders of the Mound. Wally bowed deeply.

The elder cocked his head and bowed in reply.

"No, Wally, it is I who should bow to you. You are the first worm to travel here from the other side of the Road. You bring us the hearts-warming news that Lawnia lives. And, I hear that you have flown! Remarkable!"

The elder bowed again, this time so low that his leaf-hat touched the ground. With his tail he reached out and gave Juniper a welcoming pat. Juniper replied with a quick nod.

"I am elder Daedal, Wally of Lawnia. Long has it been since we had a visitor from your village. We are elated to hear that Lawnia escaped the horror of the Great Scraping. I have been told of your challenging journey, and I request that you regale us with your tale, after you have rested and eaten of course. But first, let me welcome you to the Magnificent Mound, the most wonderful city in Worm World!"

Before Wally could reply, they turned into the tunnel, where he met another worm. She was an albino night crawler, with white glossy skin that showed smooth muscles underneath. When she spoke the sound was in the slow, soft manner of a night crawler, but to Wally it came out sweet like a rotten blade of grass.

"Young Wally, you have travelled far and risked all to be with us. Feel safe here in our Mound, amongst your own kind and in the friendship of the June bug clan. I am Diaphany, and I will be your guide while you are with us. Squirm with me and I will show you our splendid city." She shifted so that Wally, elder Daedal and Juniper could move past her into the tunnel.

Elder Daedal whispered something into Juniper's ear. Juniper turned towards Wally. "Wally, enjoy your tour of the Mound while elder Daedal and I speak on important matters."

Before Wally could disagree, Juniper and Elder Daedal moved into another tunnel and disappeared.

Chapter Eighteen
Truly Magnificent

As Wally and Diaphony moved up the tunnel, she pointed out details of the Magnificent Mound. "The Mound is constantly changing. It is layered like an onion. These layers move down as new food is added to the top and castings are taken from the bottom. While new food is exciting, most of us prefer to forage for our food from a few layers down where it is decently decayed. I prefer layer five, where it steeps and marinades to a slimy perfection. Not too watery, with a worthwhile whiff of decomposition."

She continued as they crawled. "The nutrients in castings help plants have bigger, brighter flowers and richer, healthier vegetables. Different plants require different nutrients, so we customize blends of castings for each type. We even create blends for sick plants, or delicate plants like orchids."

They passed a hollow where groups of worms were gathered around small piles of food, each pile having different selections of rotten vegetables or fruits or clippings.

Diaphony slowed for a moment and all the worms stopped mid-munch, staring at Wally. They began talking in a low murmur, heads bobbing and tails pointing. Diaphony nodded to them.

"This is one of Quidnunc's latest ideas. She calls it a Blender Bar. Instead of mixing castings at the bottom of the Mound, she has Tiger worms push portions of the right ingredients into piles and then invites worms to dine. Their castings are ready made with the right recipe!"

They continued up the tunnel. Each time they squirmed past a different group, the worms would stop to stare at Wally and then break into excited whispers. In Lawnia, Wally had gotten used to the whispers and stares as he dragged his hurt backside behind him. But now, his newly-growing tail allowed him to squirm straight and smooth, so he wondered what they were looking at.

"As you can see, we have every type of worm in the Mound," Diaphony continued. "Angleworms, garden worms, manure worms, topsoil worms, subsoil worms, night crawlers. Each has a different purpose, depending upon their special skills. For example, Tiger worms tackle the hardest and roughest pieces of food, like corn cobs and pineapple stems. They are also soldier worms...when we need them to be. You don't want to grapple with one. June bug grubs also help the Tiger worms – they especially enjoy roots and twigs."

They passed three worms daintily eating the slimy edge of a rose petal. They stopped chewing and their mouths dropped open as Wally passed.

Diaphony smiled at them and then turned to Wally in a silvery whisper.

"The opposite of Tiger worms are grey worms – they like only the most sophisticated foods like flowers, coffee grounds and tea bags. Their castings are so potent and fine that they are used very sparingly."

They came into what Diaphony called the Great Hall, a massive domed room in the center of the mound. It was so wide that Wally could not see the other side. One hundred worms stacked on top of each other would *still* not touch the ceiling. The ceiling itself was made of decomposing food, hanging in great green or brown or multicolored clumps that would periodically break free and fall to the floor in a great "splat." Small groups of worms would squirm in a mad rush to reach them and pick from the choicest chunks. With each splatter the air would stir, and Wally's skin breathed in the seductive scents of mush and rot. Spiced in were scents that Wally had never sensed before, but somehow he knew what they were – musk melon, artichoke, and lemon rind. He loved the scent of limp lemon rind, so sweet and sour at the same time!

The room was wriggling with worms. All types and sizes were represented, but more interesting to Wally were the ways the worms had decorated themselves. Some had painted their bodies in various colors – red and black from berry juice, bright green from leaves, and even a dusted gold color from flower pollen. A few worms had pieces of clothing made from seed shells and slips of woven grass. One worm had a clinging wrap that was transparent. It was wound so tightly that his face had turned blue, and he fainted to the floor when Wally smiled at him.

Here and there were worms trading exotic trinkets. One had bright green and orange pieces of plastic thread. Another had thick metal disks, the largest of which was twice the size of a coiled red wiggler like Wally. Each disk had the head and torso of a human on one side and intricate carvings on the other. Some were brownish while others were shiny silver. Yet another worm had a plastic tab with a hole on one side that she wore as a necklace. Wally wondered how she squirmed wearing that!

Wally and Diaphony passed a troupe of entertainers throwing objects into the air. They moved so quickly that there were always multiple items aloft at any time, and catching them took great skill and coordination. First they started with corn kernels, which were difficult since each worm used his center for a base while balancing with his head. He then wrapped his tail around the kernel and threw it into the air. Wally stopped to watch as they progressed to small stones then pieces of crushed glass, each wrapping his tail in a locust tree leaf for protection.

Many more worms entered the hall while Wally was watching the juggling worms. One Fat head worm came up beside Wally and Diaphony.

"Wally, this is Oneiric," said Diaphony. "He is the Master Molder of the Mound. It is his job to envision new spaces and tunnels in the Mound and help the tunneling teams form them."

Oneiric touched his forehead to the damp earth. "I am honored to meet such a renowned traveler."

Wally blushed. He had never dreamed about visiting the Magnificent Mound, yet here he was. And, by the way they were treating him, it seemed that they did not get many visitors from far away.

Diaphony continued. "The Mound is the most diverse worm habitat in Worm World. Every worm here is specialized in some way. Fat head worms like Oneiric tend to become elders or leaders because they have quick minds and long memories. Brown worms concentrate on building small tunnels, while night crawlers are used on large tunnels and halls."

Oneiric laughed. "But no matter what job we do, all of us still eat for a living!"

Before Oneiric could continue, a buzz emanated from a tall tunnel entering the Great Hall. A long parade of worms squirmed in, the lead worms waving banners of red fern leaves. Next were rows of segmented worms that made different thrumming sounds by stretching apart their segments and letting them slap back together. In the middle were three fat silkworms spinning small balloons that the inchworms behind them would bat into the crowd with their tails. Following them, rows and rows of red wiggler worms progressed, their high voices singing a lilting song. It was difficult to make out the words, but Wally thought he heard something about "salvation" and "redemption." Next was a band of mixed insects, each with a unique instrument that contributed to the music – worms tapping on taut pieces of fiber stretched between the "Y" in small twigs, beetles clacking their shells with their antennae, ants walking on their hind legs and slapping small bits of quartz together, pill bugs rubbing sticks across each other's backs.

At the rear of the procession were seven older worms sitting on willow leaves. They were being pulled by dung beetles with deep black shells and wide, flat feet. Announcing their arrival were seven red horned beetles, blowing a marching tune through their horns. Oneiric nudged him as they passed. "That is the Council of Elders, Wally."

The first elder was Daedal, who was wearing a robe made of a color photo from a human newspaper and a hat of yellowish clear film. Four of the other elders were fat head worms, each dressed in robes made of different materials such as corn husk and palm frond. One was a red wiggler. Her midsection was covered in tiny pinecone scales that shifted as she moved. A single pink rose petal cupped her head. As she passed Wally she nodded at him. The final elder was a massive red night crawler who wore only a scar down one side of his body. Bringing up the rear was Juniper, who smiled mischievously at Wally.

To Wally's surprise the procession turned directly towards him. The sea of worms parted to clear a large open space and the lead dung beetle pulled elder Daedal in front of Wally. As he did so, the seven red horned beetles finished their marching tune with a regal "dat da da da!" Elder Daedal removed his hat with his tail in a flourish and swayed his head low in the formal worm greeting.

Two Tiger worms with muscular bands rolled a hollowed acorn in front of Elder Daedal. The elder leaned forward and spoke through a hole that had been poked in the acorn's tip. His voice boomed over the crowd.

"Welcome to the Magnificent Mound, Wally of Lawnia, traveler extraordinaire, chastiser of Chumbucket, master of earth and sky, and liberator of the Bucket Brigade! Welcome Hero of Worm World!"

Chapter Nineteen
Hesitant Hero

Juniper scuttled over and lifted Wally on his shoulders so that he could be seen above the crowd. Elder Daedal continued. "This is a Son of Lost Lawnia, who has overcome great obstacles to reach us. Not only did he cross the Road, survive the Crow, and swim the Stream. He also foiled Chumbucket and, in an unprecedented feat, tricked the human boy into returning a full bucket of our red wigglers to the Mound...without a single one harmed!"

Elder Daedal waved his tail and a host of red wiggler worms squirmed into the space. They filed past Wally in a single line, each giving him a light tail slap and saying things in their funny accent like "Thanks Mate" and "Good to see you alive, brother!" and "You are my personal hero, friend!"

Wally was shocked. Everybody was staring at him, so he timidly waved his tail stub to them. Thankfully, Elder Daedal began talking again.

"All of these are remarkable, nearly unbelievable accomplishments. But there is more! Never in the history of wormkind has a worm flown and lived to tell about it!"

As he spoke a group of Thespian worms moved into the center of the clear space and acted out the elder's words. The young worm that played Wally had a strand of dried corn silk wrapped around his tail to signify Wally's damaged backside. Elder Daedal spoke slowly and clearly, pausing between each sentence to allow the actors to play their parts.

"Wally first left the ground when he saved a youngling from a Ripper Robin. He was thrown into the air by a wild peck!" The crowd murmured its approval as the young Thespian was lifted in the air by his peers and spun around.

"Then he was plucked from the searing pavement of the Road by our nemesis the Crow." The gathering gasped so hard a gust blew through the room.

"Through his wit and cunning, he confused the Crow and managed to escape – only to be plucked from the ground by the human boy and placed with this group of red wigglers into a bucket." He pointed to the area at his side where the red wigglers, now known as the Bucket Brigade, had gathered. They were demonstrating a cluster ball while chanting "Wally! Wally! Wally!"

"They are witnesses to all that happened next." The crowd shifted anxiously, and applauded at key points as the actors played out the events.

"Remarkably, Wally flew again! Chosen by the human boy from amongst his fellow red wigglers, he was skewered by the hook and cast into the stream!" The Thespians hung the actor playing Wally on a bent twig and threw him a short distance into the air. The other worms were stunned – very few had ever seen a worm with its entire body away from the ground and many believed that if a worm lost touch with the earth it would immediately die. Youngling Thespians played the parts of the little fish, as others grouped together under a yellow birch leaf to play the part of Chumbucket. A separate group pulled a hollowed, half grapefruit on top of itself and played the part of Grandfather.

Elder Daedal continued. "At great risk to himself he convinced Chumbucket to rally against the human boy." The actors pantomimed the first plan to have Chumbucket fool the boy while Grandfather rushed out of the water at him. From far out in the crowd large balls of crushed paper were thrown at the actors under the grapefruit peel as Elder Daedal told of how the boy regained his composure and attacked Grandfather with rocks.

"When this plan backfired, Wally improvised. He attached the hook to the snapping turtle's shell and the human boy was pulled into the water!" The actors threw a mushroom with pinecone seeds stuck along its front into the air. It looked strikingly like a baseball cap. When select worms waved small pieces of foil, the effect was of rippling water. The entire gathering got into the moment, making splashing sounds and moving in waves.

"After he was pulled into the water he quit fishing and returned the Bucket Brigade to the Mound, safe and sound!"

Elder Daedal paused, swaying his head slowly from side to side as they all roared and cheered. A wave of his tail brought silence, and he proceeded in a gruff whisper.

"Wally was still attached to the hook. His backside had been damaged during the Great Scraping, or as the denizens of Lawnia refer to it, Digger Day. On a rare occasion one of us will lose our backside when attacked by a mole or a bird. But Wally's backside was not separated from him on Digger Day, it was only damaged. He was forced to drag this hurt hind end around with him, disfigured." The crowed reacted with a sigh of sympathy.

"But what makes a hero is his ability to break through whatever barriers are placed in his way. At the point when his skin was saturated, when his last breath was taken, when all hope seemed lost, Wally tore himself away from the horrible hook, away from his damaged backside. So moved were the minnows of the stream that they carried him to the safety of the shore." The actor playing Wally was picked up by the crowd and passed overhead until he was placed in front of Juniper. He bowed to Wally, who was still sitting on Juniper's shoulders. Elder Daedal concluded his story.

"As luck would have it, they deposited him near our master of eloquence, Juniper, who was Wally's steward for the remainder of his perilous journey to us." Wally felt Elder Daedal's tail swirl around behind him and tap Juniper on his foreleg. Juniper's wings erupted and lifted them off the ground. All the worms inhaled at this sight. The sound of air through their skin made a loud shushing noise and for a moment all was quiet. Elder Daedal took full advantage of this pause and leaned his face back to the acorn.

"My dear citizens of the Mound, I give to you the Founder of Flight, the Benefactor of the Bucket Brigade, the Lion of Lawnia...Wonderful Wally the Worm!"

Chapter Twenty
Questions – and Answers

Wally awoke slowly, letting the coolness of the earth infuse his body. Memories of the previous day came flooding back. The crowd had rushed him, trying to touch him – a flying worm. Concerned that Wally would get hurt, Juniper had flown higher, fluttering over their heads in tight tilted circles so the crowd could see Wally better. Then Juniper escaped with Wally up a hidden shaft in the ceiling. They were exhausted from their incredible day and afraid of more crowds, so they left the Mound and rested beneath a windblown newspaper at the base of the rock wall.

Wally wrapped a piece of damp newspaper around his head. He relaxed in a coil, watching Juniper. He was sitting at the other end of the newspaper, chewing it slowly and periodically mumbling a word to himself. His head jerked up. "Insuperable! That fits you perfectly Wally!"

Wally looked at him. "What does it mean?"

"Well," replied Juniper, "like the human explorer described in the story I am eating, it means 'unable to be overcome'."

Wally thought about "insuperable" for a while. Juniper was right; he had been through many trials yet still made it to the Magnificent Mound. But, he could not have done it without help. Especially from Juniper. It seemed like they had always known each other.

"I would only agree with you if you said 'inseparable,' my friend," Wally replied with a slight grin.

Juniper's carapace shifted its rainbow colors ever so slightly, and he turned his head away. Wally guessed this was a June bug blush.

"We should be getting back to the Mound, Wally," Juniper replied. "You are a celebrity now, and I am sure the Elders will have planned plenty of appearances for you."

The entire Mound was wriggling with energy. Those thousand or so worms lucky enough to witness the parade quickly had spread the word of Wally and his incredible journey from Lawnia. Now tens of thousands of worms were talking about him, wishing to know more of his story. Every worm wanted to meet the flying hero.

Quidnunc met Wally and Juniper at the entrance tunnel, and she told them about their plans for the day. At the first event, the Elders officially removed Lawnia from the List of Lost Lands. Wally said a few quick words, and the crowd cheered. He felt his hearts slow with sadness as he thought of how Dampnia, Rotten Log, Leafy Hollow and

Flowergarden still remained on the List. Wally answered a few questions about Lawnia, and then their questions focused on flying.

"What is the view like? Does your skin dry out from the wind? What about the Sun?" and "Aren't you afraid to fly?" When they asked this last question they looked at Juniper as if they were seeing him for the first time. A June bug flying seemed strange enough to them, since of all the June bugs in the Mound, only Juniper flew frequently. But the thought of a worm flying *on* a June bug was a revelation, both exciting and frightening.

The day went on forever, with event after event. One moment Wally was receiving a garland of soft white flower petals from the Lady Land Crawlers, the next he was speaking to a luncheon of the Red Wigglers Society, and the next receiving cheers from Worms of Hope, a group that had been tireless in their assertion that Lawnia still existed.

Over the next few days they visited the Mound for a routine of appearances and questions, each night retreating to their spot near the rock wall. Eventually the appearances lessened, and Wally was given a chance to wander around the Mound. Wally found that, in the few times when he was without Juniper or any of the Elders, most worms did not recognize him. It was in one of these special times that he found a small park near the center of the Mound.

The park was both entertaining and educational. It was called "Our Story Place" and consisted of a large open room full of mushrooms – small, flat pink cups that caught drops of water from the ceiling, medium brown umbrellas that grew on tall thin stalks, and large spotted button mushrooms that smelled of warm rain and gave off a green glow that filled the room. In the center of the space was a cardboard box that had been turned on its side as a stage. Wally could just decipher the faint "Raisins" printed on its side (Juniper had been teaching Wally to read a little each night!)

The park was alive with activity, and the stage was crowded with the cast of Thespian worms that had performed on his first day at the Mound. Beside the stage was a coiled Legend worm, who told stories of the history of the Mound.

They performed a public service message consisting of a series of skits addressed to the younglings who were lounging about the space. The Legend worm narrated the scenes as the troupe of Thespians moved about the stage, acting them out. At the end, the Legend worm talked about civic duty.

"The Mound is a symbiotic city. This means that its success depends upon all worms, June bugs and other insects working together and the entire Mound collaborating with the Farmer. We each have a role to play. What is yours?"

Wally wondered. *What role can I play?* On the way back to the rock wall with Juniper, Wally contemplated this question.

It was a cloudless, moonless night, perfect for gazing at the stars. Juniper tipped himself over and practiced words to describe the night sky. "Supernal.

That means that it comes from the heavens." He scratched his antennae against his head. "Phenomenal. That means, well, pretty much fantastic."

Wally half listened to Juniper as he thought about the worms he had met that day. He had spoken at a luncheon for the Mound Movers, a group of stocky grey wigglers who were responsible for removing dirt from collapsed tunnels. They asked so many questions about flying that he was almost tired of thinking about it. Almost, but not quite. In fact, the thought of flying was always on his mind, and he realized how his fellow worms were missing out. After dwelling on this concept for a while, he came to believe that flying was a deep desire for many worms. That they shared a common need to be more than what they were – more than an animal whose body continually hugged the earth. One whose spirit soared. In a quiet moment as Wally and Juniper lay staring up at the sky, a thought struck Wally. *Any worm can fly. All it takes is a June bug.* Wally gazed at the stars and he considered the idea of any worm flying. Many questions flooded his mind, and he struggled to work through them.

He started with the bigger questions. Why were there villages anyway? Well, because worms were slow-moving creatures who couldn't cross places where there wasn't soft earth to crawl on or through. Small streams, deep rooted trees, pockets of gravel, large rocks... all of these things separated worm communities into villages. Only the most daring of worms travelled between worm villages. After Digger Day, his village had been cut off entirely. But what if *all* worms could fly? Then villages would not be so separated. A whole new world would open for wormkind. But how could he enable all worms to fly?

He knew there must be an answer. Wally stared hard at the stars. Each of the insects in the Mound had a specific role to play. How did they choose these? And why were they destined to do only this role their entire lives? He thought about the Walk Watchers in Lawnia. Before Digger Day there had been no sidewalk, therefore there were no Walk Watchers. Worms had to learn this new skill and the village had grown, had changed. So, change could be a good thing.

What if more June bugs could help worms fly? What if a whole host of June bugs carried worms wherever they wanted to go? If Juniper traveled long distances, why couldn't any June bug do the same? Wally envisioned this new way of travel. No longer would worms be limited to the small area near their birthplace. With June bugs helping, they could fly anywhere.

"Juniper," Wally asked carefully, "why are you the only June bug at the mound who flies?"

Juniper breathed in slowly then whistled through his mandibles. "Well, I'm not the only June bug who *can* fly. All of us can. It's just that my brothers and sisters all have responsibilities at the Mound, and they get all the food they need there. So, they don't need to fly. I am the restless one. I am the explorer."

He paused for a moment and made an Mmmmm sound. "I am always seeking new words to eat." He kicked one leg and spun his body so that he was looking directly at Wally. "Nobody has ever wanted to wander with me before. That is, before I met you."

Wally leaned close to Juniper. "My friend, I have an incredible idea."

Chapter Twenty One
Preparation

Wally and Juniper proceeded with utmost secrecy. After all, an idea this big would change the lives of worms everywhere. That night they developed a detailed plan. Each had a list of items to do, and over the next few days they tackled their tasks with abandon.

For a while they barely saw each other; Juniper was secretly meeting with June bug after June bug. Wally stayed behind to make preparations. The Elders had offered Wally his choice of homes within the Mound. All were surprised when Wally chose a large, abandoned castings room at the very bottom of the Mound, facing the Farmer's beet field. It was perfect for their purpose, with high ceilings and small side rooms where different castings had been held before mixing. A series of large openings led to the outside, most with flaps of wilted tobacco leaf acting as doors. When Elder Daedal joked that he could host a party for a thousand worms in his home, Wally feared that he had figured out their plan. But then the Elder had commented that Wally was a hero with many thousands of friends, so his choice of homes shouldn't surprise anybody. Maybe his home wasn't a surprise, but his plan would be!

During the day, when the sun was shining brightly and most worms stayed inside, Juniper gave flight training to the June bugs that had joined their venture. Juniper separated them into two groups – the larger bugs would carry full grown worms, the smaller would give shorter rides for the younglings. Most had never flown, but all took to the sky easily.

Wally chuckled when Juniper had them all take off simultaneously, the sky sparkling and humming with their throbbing gossamer wings. They had the same rainbow effect to their shells that Juniper did, but each had a slightly different shade to its shell, making the sky a collection of moving colors. Once they had mastered the basics, Wally worked with them individually, teaching each the cues and commands that he and Juniper had developed. He flew with each of them so they could get used to weight on their back and a tail wrapped around their carapace.

Each night he and Juniper went back to the rock wall and relaxed under the stars, talking about their new venture and making plans. As usual, Juniper flipped on his back, reciting adjectives to describe the night sky.

One night Wally stared at the twinkling stars, thinking. Now that he could fly, he could travel back to Lawnia. He imagined how everybody would greet him. How Uncle Mort would be so surprised to see him alive. How amazed they would be that he could fly. He thought of the effect flying would have on Worm World. Soon all worms would enjoy the ability to visit relatives and villages everywhere. The Great Divide would separate them no longer. The wonders of the Magnificent Mound could be shared by all. Then he thought about his parents. All the flying in the world would not bring them back.

"Juniper?" asked Wally. "You never told me what happened to your mother."

Juniper was quiet for a few moments. He spun back and forth, his eyes glistening. Then he swallowed slowly. "After I had eaten my way into the watermelon, I poked my head out to call to her. But the melon was already on the tractor, and she was left behind. My poor mother was too weak to fly. The last I saw of her, she was laying amongst the straw in the back of the truck as it pulled away onto the road." He hung his head and his wings made a light buzzing sound under his shell.

Wally's hearts sagged. "I know how you feel, Juniper, seeing somebody you love taken away and not being able to do anything about it."

"Look at us, being sad!" Juniper spun himself around and managed to flip himself back over by catching one of his legs on the rock overhang. He nudged Wally with his shoulder. "We are on the cusp of something great, Wally. Worms across the Farm will be able to see each other any time they want. Think of it! Reuniting families. Seeing far off places. Crossing The Divide!"

The next morning, when they arrived at Wally's home, Quidnunc was waiting for them.

"Wally, Elder Daedal has asked to see you. They have called a special meeting of the Council of Elders. He looked … upset." She swung her head slowly near the ground and would not look directly at him.

Wally stole a sideways glance at Juniper, who responded with a look of surprise and concern. Juniper moved his face in front of Quidnunc. "My dear, have you any idea what this meeting might be about?"

Quidnunc turned away, but wound up looking directly at Wally. "Well, there is a buzz amongst our cousins that you and Wally are working on a fantastic idea. Some have even mentioned flying. And, well…." She shuffled backward.

Juniper moved with her and locked his eyes on hers. "And how might the Elders have heard of this?" he said with a soft tone. "Might one of us been talking a little too much to her friends?"

Wally interrupted. "That's okay Juniper. The word was bound to get out sooner or later. We are ready to begin our venture, so it is fortunate that we have this occasion to speak with the Elders."

The Council room was deep at the bottom of the Mound. Unlike the rest of the city, it was not a place that constantly changed as the ceilings and walls of decaying food were eaten. Instead, it was made entirely of smooth river stones. The entrance was high and broad, with a limp purple rhubarb leaf door pulled to one side. The room had a wonderful smell, something like rotting mint. In the center was a series of hollowed half walnut shells arranged in a semicircle. Coiled inside each shell was an Elder, who used the shell as a chair. The center chair housed Elder Daedal and he motioned Wally and Juniper into the room with a smile and a warm wag of his tail. Wally noticed the red wiggler Elder looking at him closely and thought he saw her smile too.

"Gentlemen," began Elder Daedal. "How are things going? We have not spoken in a while." Juniper and Wally glanced at each other then shifted nervously.

"We have been quite busy sir," replied Wally. "Attending meetings, making plans– things like that."

Elder Daedal eyed him suspiciously. "Maybe, getting ready for a grand party in that new home of yours?"

Wally did not want to lie. "No, sir, not exactly. You see, sir, we have been working on a venture."

One of the fat head worms leaned forward in her shell so that it rocked slightly back and forth. She was wearing a scrap of cloth that had bits of quartz embedded in it, and it glittered as her chair moved. "Ah, a venture. Not an *ad*venture, but a venture you say? Might it have anything to do with the reduction in our mixed castings production because some of the June bugs are not getting proper sleep?"

"Now, now Corusca, there is no need to be so direct my dear." Elder Daedal lightly extended his tail so that it touched the front of her shell and stopped its rocking. "Wally, Elder Corusca is wondering why many June bugs are spending so much time with you and Juniper. We have heard rumors that they are flying. Not that we have anything against their flying, but you must understand what would happen if all June bugs decide to change their role in the Mound. No castings would be collected. No castings would be mixed. No piles would be created for the Farmer."

Another of the fat worms spoke. "And do you know what will happen then? No more food will be put on top of the Mound. Our wonderful city will waste away. Where will we go? What will we do?" The other Elders squirmed nervously. The fat worm next to her spoke up. "You are right, Panjandra. And, even more importantly, what will we all eat?"

Wally had not thought of these issues. His mind spun. All he wanted was to help other worms to fly. Now they were telling him his idea might threaten the very foundation of the Magnificent Mound. Luckily, Juniper replied.

"Dear Elders," he began. "Our venture *is* an adventure. It is born out of the fulfillment of a dream and its purpose is to fulfill that dream for others."

Wally regained his composure and took it from there. "All my life I have wanted to fly. But like many other things, such as resisting a Robin, leaving Lawnia, challenging the Crow and talking to a turtle, I never expected it to happen. Now, thanks to Juniper, I can fly whenever I want. I can travel to places other worms never dreamed of going." He paused and slowly scanned the Elders.

"Until now."

They all turned to look at each other, the red wiggler and night crawler leaning together to whisper. Their movements caused their seats to tilt in different directions, and the effect was one of confusion – made even worse by the formality of the room and their elaborate garb. Elder Daedal used his tail to still their seats and return composure to the room. He cleared his throat and leaned towards Juniper and Wally, speaking in a slow and measured tone.

"Are you saying that you plan to help other worms fly?"

For painful moments the room was still and silent. The elders fixed their gaze on Wally.

Wally had never considered that anybody could be against his idea. Now he was afraid of what the elders were thinking. He hesitated, then nodded.

The elders shattered the silence, bursting forth with questions and comments.

"What an interesting idea!"

"But how will he do it?"

"With June bugs, of course!"

"Who will do the work of the June bugs? How will the castings get gathered and mixed?"

They twisted in their chairs and argued back and forth, with the red wiggler and night crawler seeming to support the idea, the four fat head worms finding fault with it, and Elder Daedal balancing between the two positions.

One fat head worm was almost yelling. "This will put the Mound into chaos. Flying worms! If we were meant to fly we would have wings." The other fat heads nodded in agreement.

The night crawler spoke over her in a booming voice. "Ferrishyn, you are wise to be concerned with what circumstances this change might bring, but you must agree that being able to fly will unite all of the villages across The Farm." Elder Ferrishyn scrunched her body in annoyance and pointed her head into the air.

Elder Daedal addressed the elders. "My dearest peers. There is no precedent for us to follow in this matter. I do not believe we can lawfully require Wally and Juniper to stop their venture. But, we are expected to act for the greater good of the Magnificent Mound and its citizens. I believe that flying will bring many new challenges, but will also confer many benefits. However, I share your hesitation with such a radical and incongruent idea."

The elders mumbled between themselves, casting frequent glances at Wally and Juniper. An ebony ant walked in front of them, carrying a white daisy with seven petals. It stopped before Elder Ferrishyn and held out the flower. She tapped it with her tail. The ant continued, stopping in front of each elder. All tapped their tails on the flower, even the red wiggler, who shook her head before doing so. At last, the ant came to the night crawler. His great size made his tail spill out of the walnut shell. The ant stood there a few moments then started shaking slightly.

That night crawler is a little scary, thought Wally.
He had heard that the night crawler was called
Wallop, and Wally did not want to find out why.

Wallop spoke to the Council. "It is our job to help
the Mound thrive. Sometimes that means we create

rules and assignments, but just as often it means that we support change. That we give the inhabitants of the Mound options and choices. For this reason, I cannot vote to limit Wally and Juniper's ad-venture. They have an ingenious idea and should be allowed to explore it!" He pulled one petal from the flower and dropped it on the ground.

Elder Daedal slid forward. "We are not unanimous." He looked at each elder slowly, nodding his head. Then he thought for a moment before continuing. "Wally and Juniper, you shall be allowed to continue your venture. However, flights will be limited to less than ten percent of all June bugs, should they wish to participate. In addition, all flights will occur in the immediate vicinity of the Mound, until such time as we can determine what effect flying will have on our society."

In unison, the elders slapped their tails on the floor three times, making a WHAP, WHAP, WHAP sound.

The ant ushered Wally and Juniper to the entrance and, with a wink, closed the purple curtain behind them.

Chapter Twenty Two
Insuperable Air

There was no need to advertise. Word spread from the moment they left the Council of Elders. Wally guessed it was the ant who leaked the story.

All worms were wondering about who would get to fly. Worms crammed into Our Story Place every hour to watch the Thespians act out Wally's adventures. At the end of each show they performed an encore in which they speculated how the whole flying idea would work.

"Will they give rides on Juniper?" yelled the Legend worm to the crowd. A large fat worm wearing a split acorn shell played Juniper, immediately appearing exasperated at the number of Thespian worms trying to climb on him. "Will they have other June bugs offering flights?" A handful of Thespians also wearing split acorns pushed through the crowd. Other Thespian worms slid on top of these, and the group made a comedy of bumping into each other.

The Legend worm continued. "But the other June bugs have never flown." His tone became low and ominous. "How will they pull it off? What daring! What courage!"

Wally and Juniper quickly realized how ambitious their plans were. The Mound held tens of thousands of worms, but they were allowed only twenty seven flying June bugs! They developed a fair method of choosing the lucky few for first flight. Oneiric helped them implement their plan and Wally's new Thespian friends at Our Story Place spread the word by adding a new encore.

The Legend worm built anticipation in the crowd, but this time he had answers. "So. . . how will they choose, you ask? Good question! Here is how, and go tell your friends!" He paused a few moments as the crowd gathered close.

"Buried in your food, in places throughout the Mound, are twenty seven silver sunflower seeds. Do not eat them! For every silver seed is a ticket. A ticket to fly!" Actors with the half acorn shells went into an intricate dance, choreographed so they each smoothly swooped by the other. The crowd cheered. "Each day twenty seven more seeds will be hidden. So if you don't find one today, then keep looking!"

"The first wave of flights begins tomorrow – so get eating!" The Legend worm waved his tail at the tunnels leading from the park. The crowd surged and headed for the exits. One red wiggler youngling was smart enough to stay put and try eating from a slop pile that had just dropped from the ceiling. Immediately he began yelling.

"I found a seed! I found a seed!"

The entire hall turned to chaos as worms stampeded to find piles to eat. That day the Mound buzzed as worms ate twice their normal allotment. Generations to come remembered the event on "Feast to Fly" day – a new worm holiday.

The lucky twenty seven were determined quickly. There were eleven red wigglers, five fat worms, six grey worms, one tiger worm, three brown worms…and one night crawler! The enormous night crawler graciously gave the silver seed to his young, and much smaller, niece.

On the evening of the first flight the entire Mound came out for the festivities. It was a carnival atmosphere, with all sorts of games, food and fun. One worm had opened a stand selling "flying fruit." He would swing his customers from a small bush by a piece of baling twine, then bat a piece of apple with his tail so they could snag it out of the air. Another was selling "cloud candies" that were really pieces of dried orange pith. One group of acrobat worms invented a new trick, in which three worms threw a balled-up forth worm into the air and he spread out to reveal a set of flower petal wings.

The largest outside door at Wally's home had been replaced by a massive mushroom cap embossed with the picture of a flying worm. The crowd packed the area outside, waiting to see what would be revealed. Here and there groups of nervous younglings were forming and reforming cluster balls.

Suddenly, a double column of stink bugs parted the crowd and made its way to the door. Each pair held a blade of wide, new grass stretched between them, with a carpenter ant walking on its hind legs and blowing on the center of the blade. The resulting trumpet sound quieted the crowd. Two giant June bugs rolled the mushroom cap aside, and Juniper walked through the door with Wally on his back.

Behind them came the Council of Elders, dressed in their finest. Next, out crawled the twenty seven winners, each wearing a harness made of woven fiber. The grass blade band blew three high notes, and through the door scuttled twenty seven June bugs. Each had a ring of fiber around its neck and a different hatched and colored pattern painted on its shell. All had broad smiles, and a few buzzed their shells with anticipation.

Elder Daedal's two Tiger worms rolled out the hollowed acorn and the elder nodded to Wally. Wally squirmed up to the shell and placed his mouth to the opening.

"Um, thank you all for coming today." The crowd cheered and he paused until they calmed down. "Inhabitants of the Magnificent Mound, I thank you for welcoming me to your city with such kindness. At hearts, I am just a regular worm from the humble village of Lawnia. I am grateful for the challenges that have been placed before me, and I have grown in ways I never thought possible. I left behind, quite literally, a piece of myself along the way. But I also lost something. My fear! Fear of trying new things. Of challenging myself. Of crossing that Divide." The crowd murmured in agreement and respect. "In fact, I found that the biggest Divide was not the road that separated Lawnia from the Magnificent Mound. Instead, it was the Divide I had inside. The fear that separated me from the worm I longed to be." Worms nodded and swayed their heads. A few "hurrah's" went through the crowd.

Wally continued. "What helped me to see my life clearly was the excitement and empowerment I found in flying. So I thought 'Why can't all worms experience the same thing?' As I discussed this idea with Juniper, we had what Juniper calls an epiphany. We realized that we had discovered the ability to help not just me, but all worms to fly!"

As he said this, Wally waved his tail and each of the twenty seven worms responded by mounting a June bug and securing its harness to the ring around the June bug's neck. The grass blade players blew a long sharp note. All the June bugs fanned their wings and hovered above the ground. Elder Daedal looked back at Wally and smiled. Then Wally slid aside and Elder Daedal leaned close to the acorn.

"So my dear denizens of Worm World, we usher in a new era for all worms. Flight!"

With that he threw his crooked leaf-hat into the air. The crowd went wild, hooting and cheering. Wally hopped onto Juniper and they shot upward. The twenty-seven June bug and worm pairs zoomed into the sky behind them.

Every day for weeks this scene repeated. Stories from the limited number of worms who were able to fly spread through the Mound like wild fire, creating a constant buzz of excitement and anticipation. The Council of Elders studied everything closely. Wherever Wally and Juniper went, they were treated with respect and admiration.

However, Wally had a lingering desire to fulfill.

The worms in the village of Lawnia were amazed one misty evening when Wally and Elder Daedal descended from the sky onto the sidewalk. Oneiric had the unique honor of carrying the elder, and Juniper could not tell which of them was having more fun. To his surprise, Wally was welcomed as a hero in Lawnia too. By sacrificing himself to save Slider from the Robin, he had been presumed dead and a memory pebble had been placed in his honor. With the news that he was alive and had conquered the sky for all wormkind, Lawnia named him its "Hero for all Time."

The flight back was one of sadness and satisfaction, revelation and relief. Just a few short weeks before, Wally had no plan for his life. Now he was co-owner of a wonderful venture, responsible for the wave of change that was sweeping over Worm World.

He had a new purpose, a new home, and thousands of new friends. And yet, without his parents, he still felt lonely.

Epilogue
Inseparable

Many days had passed since Wally and Juniper had returned to the Mound with Elder Daedal and Oneiric. Their venture had taken on a life of its own, and Wally and Juniper now could relax and fly for fun.

Late one hazy afternoon, Wally coiled beneath the overhang at his favorite place near the rock wall. Juniper lay lazily upside down near him, occasionally spinning himself around with his foreleg. The Sun shone on them, but at this time of day its rays were not harmful. Wally had learned to live with the Sun, at times soaking in its warmth before returning to the cool darkness underground.

Their stillness was broken by the buzz of Oneiric's wings as he landed lightly, leaving Elder Daedal on the ground beside Wally. Oneiric fluidly flipped Juniper right side up. He whispered in Juniper's ear, and both shot into the sky. Wally and Elder Daedal sat in silence for a spell, washed by the orange sky.

Elder Daedal turned to Wally. "My boy, there is something I think you should know. Periodically, I have a chance to communicate in some detail with Farmer. He informs me of happenings across the Farm. This morning he shared news so important that it could affect all of Worm World." Wally uncoiled so that he could see Elder Daedal's face. "He told me that all the soil scraped away during Digger Day was saved and then later used to make the lawns for the new human houses along the Road." He sat silently, waiting to see Wally's reaction to this news.

Wally's mind raced. "Are you saying that the worms taken might be alive?" He shook his head in disbelief. "That my parents might be alive?" Elder Daedal smiled. Wally was so stunned that he did not see Juniper land beside him.

"So all I need to do is go out there and find them?" His five hearts raced.

Juniper smiled. "My friend, all *we* need to do is go find them. And I am sure we will also find many other missing worms along the way."

Juniper leaned into Wally. "No better time than the present to get started, I suppose."

Still in shocked silence, Wally slid onto Juniper and the two lifted off. Elder Daedal and Oneiric waved after them.

Finally Wally found his voice. "Juniper, do you really think we will find my parents?"

Juniper clacked his mandibles. "Well Wally, you will have a splendid story to tell them. You are a hero, so I have to believe your parents are made of the same strong stuff." He nodded. "Yes, I do believe we will find them."

Wally stared at the horizon as they flew into the evening sky.

And the setting Sun seemed to smile.

About the Author

When it is wet outside, DJ Michaud can be found rescuing Wally's from his driveway. He believes everybody can fly, if just given the chance.

You can find out more about him at www.djmichaud.com.

Glossary

Abandon – to give (oneself) over to natural impulses, usually without self-control

Abridged – shortened by taking pieces out while keeping the basic contents

Abrupt – sudden or unexpected

Abundant – present in great quantity

Account – an oral or written description of particular events or situations; a narrative

Acrobat – a skilled performer of gymnastic feats

Adjectives – words used to describe a noun

Afford – to be able to pay for

Airstream – the rush of air as a car drives by

Albino – having pale or whitish skin

Alliance – a treaty of cooperation between groups

Allotment – a share of something

Allowed – permitted to happen

Aloft – in the air

Alternately – to change back and forth

Altitude – extent or distance upward; height

Amazed – greatly surprised

Ambitious – desiring success

Amphibian – an animal that can live both on land and in the water

137

Antennae – two antenna, as on the head of an insect

Anticipation – with expectation or hope

Anxious(ly) – full of mental distress or uneasiness

Any worm – a worm's way of saying "anybody"

Appreciate – to value highly

Apprehension – anticipation of misfortune

Approached – came up to; moved towards

Arduous – requiring much energy; full of hardships

Array – a large and impressive grouping

Asphalt – black tar used to pave roads

Assertion – a statement or declaration, often without support or reason

Atmosphere – mood or emotional tone; environment

Awash – crowded or full of

Bait – something used as a lure in fishing

B'next – Commander Alexander's way of saying "beside"

Baling twine – the string used to tie a bale of hay

Bane – death; destruction; ruin

Barbed – having barbs or sharp points

Barbs – the pointed parts of a fishhook

Behemoth – a creature of monstrous size or power

Befell – came upon

Benefactor – a kindly helper

Bicker – normally means to argue, but in our story it is the Commander's word for a hind end

Blendings – what the worms call different mixes of castings

Blissfully – happily

Bloke – a male friend

Blot out – to cover up

Bobbing – moving in short jerky motions

Bosom – a mother's chest

Bound – I use this word in two ways. One is "likely to happen" and the other is "on the way to somewhere"

Bounded – surrounded by

Bounty – a plentiful amount

Brethren – brothers and sisters

Brilliant – smart

Bucko – buddy

Bulbous – bulb shaped or bulging

Bunged – injured or damaged

Canopy – leafy branches

Carapace – the hard shell making up the chest of certain animals

Carcass – anything from which the life and power is gone – in this case a dried dandelion

Castings – worm poop, but in reality worm poop is more like dirt than poop

Cattail – a reed-like plant that grows in marshy areas with a tall stock with a long, brown spike

Celerity – swiftness, speed

Centerpiece – the central or outstanding point or feature

Certainly – definitely going to happen

Challenge – I use this word both as a verb (summon to face a test) and as a noun (something that takes special effort to overcome)

Chastiser – person (or worm in our case) who provides discipline or punishment

Chord – a feeling or emotion

Choreographed – well planned movement

Chortles – gleeful chuckles

Civic duty – responsibilities of each citizen in a community

Cinch – easy to do

Clinging – closely sticking too

Cluster – a group of worms close together

Cockleburr – a coarse weed, and one of our character's names (I added an extra "r")

Codgered – while the word "codger" means a grumpy old man, in my book it is a term that the Commander uses to mean "messed up"

Collaborate – to work together

Collegiate – intended for use by college students

Column – individuals walking in a long narrow line

Commotion – a disturbance or disorder

Companion – a friend

Composed (of) – made of

Compost – a mixture of decaying organic substances

Composure – self controlled state of mind

Concentrate – to focus on

Confer – to give

Conflicted – having differing emotions at the same time

Connoisseur – a person with fine taste who likes trying new things

Conquered – overcome by force

Consuming – eating

Contemplated – thought about

Conversed – spoke together

Convulsions – rapid movements of one's body

Coordination – interacting in an orderly and pleasing way

Corkscrew – a spiral

Corkscrewed – flew in a spiral

Corusca – is a name of one of the Elders. It is derived from the word coruscate, which means to sparkle and gleam.

Craw – the stomach of an animal

Crystallizing – forming and becoming hard and clear

Critical – of key importance

Cue – a signal to take an action

Cunning – showing intelligence in action

Curiosity – desire to learn or know about something

Cusp – the point of change

Daedal – skillful; ingenious – I felt this made a great name for a leader of worms.

Debt – something that is owed to another

Decayed – rotted

Decently – well done

Decipher – to figure out (in this story, it means to "barely be able to read" the word Raisins)

Decomposition – the process of rotting

Deed – something that is done or performed

Deem – determine, define

Deliberate – carefully paced and purposeful

Delivered – brought into or carried to

Denizen – inhabitant; worms who live in a certain area

Descending – moving downward

Desperately – with an urgent need

Destiny – something that is about to happen; for Juniper it meant his future life

Determination – with fixed intent

Developed – created

Devious – shifty or crooked

Diaphanous – almost completely transparent. I created the name Diaphony from this word.

Digestive – breaking down food in one's stomach

Dimwitted – not very smart

Dine – eat

Directly – straight towards

Disbelief – refusing to believe that something is true

Discomfort – mild pain or lack of comfort

Disfigured – deformed or blemished

Disgruntled – not satisfied

Diverse – made of various kinds

Domain – area or region

Domed – shaped like an upside-down bowl

Drastic – more extreme than normal

Drawl – to speak in a slow manner

Dumbfounded – made speechless with surprise

Dumbstruck – similar to dumbfounded

Ebony – black

Edible – able to be eaten

Efficacious – very effective

Efficient – performing with the least waste of effort

Elaborate – worked out with great care and many details

Elated – happy

Eloquence – using language with skill and persuasion

Emanated – came from

Embarrassed – uncomfortable with one's self

Embossed – printed with a raised surface

Empowering – to supply with ability and power

Empowerment – the act of empowering

Encountered – came across

Endured – continued to exist despite something

Energetic – powerful in action or effect

Energizing – giving energy

Enormous – very great in size

Entanglement – twisted together in a bad situation

Enticing – attractive

Entrée – the food in the main course of a meal

Entwine – to wrap around

Eventually – after a while

Envisioned – pictured in one's mind

Epilogue – a concluding part added to a book. In the case of Wally, I felt it was important that the reader have hope about finding Wally's parents.

Epiphany – insight into the greater meaning of something, usually caused by a simple experience

Euphoric – feeling of happiness and confidence

Exaggerate(d) – overstated; bigger than normal

Excitement – a state of heightened happiness and expectation

Exhalation – breathing out

Exasperated – irritated or annoyed

Exotic – excitingly not normal

Expanse – spread out over a large area

Expectantly – with much hope or anticipation

Extensive – far reaching; comprehensive

Extraordinaire – uncommon, remarkable

Fabricated – made up

Fabulous – exceptionally good

Fascinating – of great interest or attention

Fanciful – imaginary and unreal

Fantastic – incredibly great

Fantastical – a version of "fantastic" that has the same meaning. I just like the sound of this word!

Fate – an unavoidable future event; something that was meant to be

Ferrishyn – this is not a real word. I made it up!

Filet – to cut up into pieces

Flit – to move lightly and swiftly; to dart about

Flourish – a grand display

Fluidly – with ease and grace

Flush – filled with energy from sudden emotion

Forage – to search for something, usually for food

Forefinger – the first finger next to the thumb

Forelegs – the front legs of an animal

Fortitude – mental and emotional strength

Fortuitously – luckily

Fortunate – lucky

Founder – an entity who starts something

Franticly – done with desperation or fear

Frequent(ly) – happening often

Froth – liquid disturbed with foamy bubbles

Garb – clothing

Garland – a wreath of flowers

Generation – the amount of time between the birth of a parent and the birth of their children

Gestation – the period of time before Juniper's mama was to lay her eggs

Glistening – having a wet-looking shine

Glitter – to sparkle with reflected light

Glossy – having a shiny or lustrous surface

Gnarly – misshapen

Gnat – a very small two winged fly

Gossamer – extremely thin and web-like

Gossip – a person who spreads idle talk or rumors

Graciously – nicely; courteously

Grand – stately, majestic, dignified

Gratitude – thankfulness

Gravelly – harsh and grating

Gravid – loaded with eggs

Gruff – harsh or rough

Guffawed – a loud and strong burst of laughter

Guidance – advice and assistance

Gullet – throat

Gyrated – spun around a center point

Happenings – events or occurrences

Harmony – the state of being orderly and pleasing

Hatched – I use this word in two ways. The first means "to bring forth from an egg" and the second means "a series of closely set parallel lines."

Haunt – remain with (and be reminded of)

Heartiest – most abundant and nourishing

Heightened – increased or strengthened

Heroic – displaying the qualities and characteristics of a hero

Hesitant – undecided or doubtful

Highlighted – made to stand out or be prominent

Hoard – a great collection

Honor(ed) – having high respect and distinction

Hooligan – somebody who is rough and mean

Horizon – the line that is the apparent boundary between earth and sky

Horrific – horrible and scary

Host – I use this word in two ways also. The first means "a great number of things or persons" and the second means "to welcome others to one's home."

Husk – the dry external covering of a fruit or vegetable

Immense – very large

Immobilize – to stop something from moving

Impaled – to pierce the body with a sharpened stake

Impenetrable – cannot be penetrated

Implement – to carry out

Incensed – made angry

Incongruent – not in agreement with the norm

Incorrigible – difficult or impossible to control

Incredible – hard to believe; astonishing

Individually – one at a time

Infuse – to soak in

Ingenious – clever and original

Inhabitants – a person or animal that lives in a place

Inhale – to breathe in deeply

Instill – to introduce by gradual, persistent efforts

Instinctively – understood naturally; unlearned

Inseparable – not able to be parted or separated

Insuperable – impossible to overcome

Intently – with sharply focused attention

Interest – engaging attention

Intermix – to mix together

Intertwined – wrapped together

Intimidating – producing fear of inferiority

Intricate – full of complexly arranged elements

Intrepid – fearless

Invigorating – filling with life and energy

Jerky – I use this word in two ways: the first means "dried meat," and the second "having sudden stops and starts"

Jostled – bumped, pushed or shoved

Jumbled – a confusing arrangement; all mixed up

Kaleidoscope – a continually changing pattern of shapes and colors

Kin – I use this word in two ways. The first means "relatives" and the second means "feeling a relationship with"

Knoll – a small rounded hill

Land Lubber – an animal that cannot leave the ground

Lavender – a pale bluish purple

Legion – a division of an army

Lethal – deadly

Liberator – somebody who sets another free

Lichen – a light green colored fungus with branch-like growths

Lilting – with a rhythmic swing

Lingering – staying in place longer than usual

Literally – without exaggeration

Livelihood – means of support

Luncheon – a formal lunch held in conjunction with a meeting

Luscious – This word I also use in two ways. The first means "luxurious" and the second means "richly satisfying"

Majestic – having a lofty dignity

Mammoth – huge

Mandible – a jaw-like mouthpiece on an insect, they come in pairs

Manicured – trimmed and well-kept

Massive – huge and heavy

Marinade – to soak food in a mixture that makes it more tender and tasty

Marvelous – superb; excellent; great

Measured – regular and uniform

Menace – something that threatens to cause harm

Mesmerized – similar to hypnotized

Mischievously – playfully teasing

Miserable – extremely unhappy

Modes – manners or methods

Morsel – a bite or mouthful

Motivate – to inspire to action

Mucker – This is a word created by Commander Alexander that means "to mess up"

Mucus – a slimy substance that worms have on their skin to protect and lubricate it

Murmur – to speak in a low tone

Navigate – to find one's way

Nervously – uneasy and with tension

Notoriously – well known for a bad quality

Nutritious – providing nourishment

Objection – a reason offered in disagreement

Objects – things

Obligatory – required by law or tradition

Obstacle – a barrier or hardship

Obstinate – stubborn

Occasion – a special or important time

Occasionally – once in a while

Ominous – sounding like the future might be bad

Oneiric – related to dreams. I chose this name because a master builder needs to be a dreamer.

Oodles – a large quantity

Oozed – slid in a slippery manner

Opportunity – a good position or chance

Orb – a sphere

Organic – made of plant material

Ostracized – excluded from a group

Overshadowed – made less important by comparison

Overwhelmed – completely overcome

Paltry – extremely small

Panjandra – This name I derived from the word Panjandrum – a self-important official.

Pantomimed – acted out with gestures but not sounds

Partake – to take part in (in this case, to eat)

Participate – to take part in

Pattering – made with a succession of light rapid sounds

Peculiar – strange or odd

Penetrate – to pierce or pass through

Peril – something that may cause injury, loss or destruction

Perilous – involving grave risk

Periodically – recurring at intervals of time

Persevering – persisting in anything undertaken

Perspective – an angle for viewing something

Phenomenal – highly extraordinary; exceptional

Phenomenon – an observed event or occurrence

Picket (as in fence) – a stake used in multiples to make a fence

Piercing – penetrating sharply

Pitch a pup – This is the Commander's way of saying "put up a tent"

Pith – the soft, sponge-like white stuff inside an orange peel

Plentiful – existing in great plenty; abundant

Plied – worked at steadily

Plowed (into) – to move forcefully into something

Plying – passing along steadily; for this story, "plying the sky" is a cute way of saying "to fly"

Precedent – example from the past to serve as a guide

Precipice – The first meaning of this word is "a cliff" and the second is "a situation of great peril"

Predicament – a difficult situation

Prefer – to like better

Presented – offered or introduced

Presumed – believed to be

Procession – a body of people moving along in an orderly manner

Prodding – poking or jabbing

Progressed – moved forward or moved on to

Prone – The first meaning is "tend to be" and the second is "lying face down"

Propelled – pushed or moved forward

Proportion – having the proper relation/ratio between portions

Pulsating – vibrating with the beat

Pupate – transforming from a larva to an insect

Purposely – done on purpose

Purposefully – done with intent

Pursuing – following closely

Quagmire – a difficult situation

Quest – an adventurous expedition

Quidnunc – somebody who likes to know the latest news; a gossip

Radical – far from normal; extreme

Raffle(d) – a lottery where you buy a ticket to possibly win a prize

Rally – to concentrate ones strength

Random – occurring without reason or pattern

Recently – happening not long ago

Reciting – listing from memory

Relative – as an adjective it means "considered in relation to something else" or as a noun it means "somebody who is related to someone else"

Relief – a feeling of ease resulting from the removal of stress

Recounted – told in detail

Recurring – happening again and again

Redemption – being rescued from a problem or mistake

Reduction – a lessening

Reedy – full of reeds

Refer – give it the name of

Regal – royal sounding; stately and splendid

Regale – entertain

Remarkable – worthy of notice or attention

Renowned – celebrated; famous

Repository – a place where things are stored

Represented – at least one from each possible group was present

Resumed – begun again

Revelation – something revealed

Rhythmically – with measured regularity

Role – a person's job or responsibility

Salvation – the act of saving or protecting from harm

Satisfaction – fulfillment and gratification

Saturated – soaked thoroughly

Savor – to allow oneself to feel the enjoyment of something

Scootle – Commander's way of saying "slide on over"

Scores – a great many in number

Scuttle – to move with quick steps

Scuttle bug – also known as a roly poly or pill bug

Secretes – pronounced "si-kreets" it means to discharge a fluid

Seductive – tempting

Select – carefully chosen

Serendipitous – lucky to be found by accident

Sesquipedalian – using long words

Shimmering – with a quivering shine

Shushing – making the sound of "shush" like when somebody tells you to be quiet

Siblings – brothers and sisters

Signify – to represent by something

Simultaneously – at the same time

Skewered – pierced through the middle

Skit – a short play or sketch

Slack – excess line

Slopchops – A word Chumbucket uses for tasty food

Slunk – crawled in fear or defeat

Slyly – playfully or mischievously

Smoldering – smoking from something burning without a flame

Smugly – confidently

Snippets – fragments or pieces

Sods – individuals

Solitude – the state of being alone

Sparingly – only a little at a time

Spindly – long, thin and frail

Spiraled – flew in a spiral

Spittle – saliva

Splendid – gorgeous; magnificent

Stampeded – rushed wildly

Steeled – prepared

Steeps – soaks in water or liquid

Strikingly – noticeably

Stunned – dazed or bewildered

Subdivision – a portion of land separated into lots for real estate development

Sublime – impressing the mind with a sense of power and awe

Succulent – rich in desirable qualities

Suddenly – happening quickly without warning

Sullen – gloomy and silent

Superb – extremely good; rich and grand

Supernal – heavenly

Superlative – of the best kind, quality or order

Supine – lying on one's back, face upward

Surreal – dreamlike, fantastic

Survey – to take a view of or to study

Suspiciously – with question or suspicion

Sustenance – nourishment; food

Swath – a long, narrow strip

Symbiotic – mutually beneficial relationship between two or more groups

Sympathy – sharing the feelings of another; having compassion

Tackle – to undertake or deal with

Taken aback – surprised

Tarmac – another word for a tarred road

Taut – tightly drawn

Terrestrial – related to the earth; for our story, it means "bound" to the earth

Thespian – an actor or actress

Thoroughly – completely and with attention to detail

Throbbing – beating with force and rapidity

Thrummed – The first meaning used is "beat" as in beating wings and the second meaning is "a sound somewhat like strumming the strings on a guitar."

Thrust to weight ratio – Juniper's strength to fly compared to how much he weighs

Thumbers – a word that one of the Bucket Brigade worm uses to mean "fingers"

Tilted – leaning to one side

Timidly – shyly

Torso – the trunk of a body

Transfixed – held motionless in amazement

Transparent – clear or see-through

Travails – pain and suffering resulting from a hardship

Traverse – to pass or move over, along or through

Treacherous – deceptive, untrustworthy or unreliable

Tremendous – extraordinarily great in size, amount or intensity

Tribulations – severe trials and suffering

Trough – pronounced "trof" it is a channel for funneling water away from the road

Troupe – a group of entertainers

Trudge – to walk wearily

Unbelievable – so remarkable as to strain belief

Undulating – moving in a wavelike motion

Unanimous – being in agreement

Unique – different from all others

Unison – "in unison" is doing something together

Unparalleled – unequaled or unmatched

Unprecedented – never happened before

Unpredictable – unable to be foreseen

Utmost – the most

Vaguely – not clearly or distinctly

Valid – true and correct

Vast – of very great area or extent

Venture – a business enterprise

Venturing – daring to go

Vibrating – moving back and forth quickly and repeatedly

Vicinity – the area or region near or about a place

Violent – rough and intense in force

Vocabularies – lists or collections of words or phrases in a given language

Whiff – a slight trace of odor or smell

Wilted – limp and drooping

Wit – understanding and intelligence

Witty – full of wit

Worthwhile – valuable or important

Writhe – to twist and squirm in pain